THE AGE OF A LOBSTER

A NOVEL

STEPHEN MATHEWS

Read me like you listen to music

THE AGE OF A LOBSTER

1

He called me *Lemon*. I didn't like it much at first – hated it, even – but I realize now that being called "Lemon" was one of the most freeing moments to ever come from my recklessness. I was eighteen and over it, but Andrew saw that there was more to me than the sour way I acted. At least I hope he did because I already bought the plane ticket to California just to be with him again.

I am twenty-three years old and have been burying people for the last five of them. The recently renovated Marlow & McClay Mortuary has become a symbol of comfort to everyone but me. I don't talk about it much, though, because I make good money and my parents are thrilled about that. And even if it's not what I wanted to do with my life, I have what it takes to be a great mortician – innate kindness, a strong sense of humor, and determined insomnia.

I have come to accept that a person is only ever going to try to improve their own circumstances when possible. We act on what we know to be true and make the decision we think is best at the time – even if it wasn't the best decision, looking back. So, as a result of their endless pursuit of a reputable life, my parents raised a reputable liar; a liar who refused to look inward on himself for the whole of twenty-three years. Minus, of course, the five or six years of childhood when self-reflection was no more than depicting "sadness" as a rain cloud scribbled in cobalt blue wax. Cobalt blue was, after all, my favorite color.

I was nine when my grandfather died. We didn't take the trip for his funeral because the business my dad started couldn't be left alone and because my mom just didn't see a point in going. I could tell that my dad *wanted* to go since he cried about it in his own silent way, but there were family dynamics that I was too young and inattentive to really understand. No one called to ask why we weren't there. Nothing arrived in the mail. All that came through was a picture of my grandfather, dead in his casket, taken on Aunt Lou's flip phone. To me, it looked like my grandfather was made out of plastic.

Wounded and pissed off, my dad called my grandmother to ask about what of his father's things were going to be sent to him. She told him "None of it," and hung up, snapping off the last branch of our extended family tree. I wasn't surprised because even though I was only nine, I wasn't completely unaware of the way people can be.

Carlos, a funeral director and only friend to my father, told us that families often turn against each other when someone dies, and that it couldn't be helped.

In response, my dad poured his entirety into his entrepreneurship. He was a self-righteous man who wrote like a poet and craved prestige, which complimented his classic and uncomplicated personality. Really, who wouldn't have trusted him as the in-demand, freelance copywriter for several Denver-based enterprises? Certainly not those who *had* to hire him (despite his costly commission) in the chance that he was to sign with a competitor. But what this "new" Jeremiah Marlow was – above all else – was his reputation, and he constantly reminded me that everything I did was a direct reflection of our family name. So much so, that my first name became the extent of my green-eyed, dirty blond identity, and "Ian" is a very short name.

Having grown up in Chicago's poverty, my mom rejoiced in my dad's high-paying reputation. He was big money. He was elite. He was the opposite of everything his own father stood for, but at least he cried when his father died, right?

It was just us three, the Marlows, who lived in a nice home nestled in the valley of a town north of Denver. There was never an issue with the holidays, we never worried about surprise visits from out-of-towners, and my dad's wealth stayed in the home. Money was the language we all spoke, and as I got older, I learned to *hate* money.

I don't remember much about my eighteenth birthday, only that I hated my body enough to leave the cake alone, and that from that point on I would be expected to make decisions for myself. Of course, this was a joke to someone like me who only ever followed what my parents wanted just to avoid further severing of the family tree stump.

That's not to say that I was always agreeable, though, as parents and I fought often, and one particular argument led to the intentional snapping in half of a laptop. But if at any point I acted against their direction, my dad would effortlessly let it slip how hard he worked to put a large sum of money aside for my college education, and that usually shut me up. And in the rare case I still had something to say, my mom reminded me that she quit her job to raise me while my dad worked. Knowing that two people had sacrificed so much just to give me my best shot at life kept me complaisant.

I understand how I did my part in creating this reality for myself, so of course I had a sour outlook. It's because of this twisted dynamic that I am *still* running a funeral home business with Robin. Robin's great, but I hate not being able to travel, which is all I want to do anyway. So, when I got a call Monday evening asking me to come back to California, I agreed without even thinking about it. Out of twenty-three years of life, it was the first decision I made with no one else in mind.

My hands are shaking because the ticket feels heavy in them and not because I'm nervous about the flight.

I compare the gate number and time to what's on the ticket – not that I need to, though, because I have an excellent memory. Gate C47 waits to welcome passengers of the 7:16 AM flight from Denver, Colorado, and deliver them to San Diego, California. The voice over the speaker announces that group B can begin boarding, so I file in line behind the others who also didn't waste their money on first-class seats like their fathers would have. Coach is just fine for those of us who have nothing left to prove to anyone. I did make sure to get a window seat, though, so I could watch the beaches of San Diego greet us. My body may be landlocked, but my mind is coastal.

After sending Robin a quick "thank you so much for holding down the fort" text, I slide my phone into my pocket and contemplate the lives of others. Flight attendants help shove personal artifacts into the overhead bins while passengers like me focus on their own individuality. So many different lives seated in a hallway of carpet and vinyl. *Are they going back for someone too?* I wonder. *Or maybe they have it figured out already and know exactly who they are and why.* I pull a small piece of paper from the inside pocket of my suit coat and unfold it for the twelfth time that morning.

With a blend of hope and helplessness, I read the handwritten list of things I want to do when I see him again:

- Return the gift
- Tell him I love him

I fold the note again, careful not to tear the edges, and return it to the pocket that sits over my heart. By closing my eyes and leaning my head into the creases of my knuckles, I can feel the world around me shifting. I smirk, thinking to myself how ridiculous it is that I'm only now about to fly for the second time in my life, and it's the exact same flight I took five years ago when I was eighteen and over it. The doors of the airplane close, and I surrender myself to memories.

2

"I don't want anything to do with California."

My parents and I were huddled around a pile of luggage – some was theirs; some was mine – and the Colorado sun had just begun to spill over the horizon in all its brilliant nonchalance. I just graduated high school and wanted more to do with my own patterns than discovering something else on the West Coast with Alli, who I was sure I wouldn't even recognize.

"Don't argue with me, Ian," my mom insisted. I winced as my dad leaned my suitcase against the muddy bumper of their newest car. I tried to load it myself, but he took over and claimed that I didn't know how to prioritize the space, which maybe I didn't, but at least I wouldn't have dried mud pressed into my suitcase's teal fibers. Honestly, cargo space wouldn't have been an issue if they would have gone back home after dropping me off at the airport. To them, though, dropping me off at the airport was just a quick stop on their way to Cherry Creek State Park, where they would spend the weekend proving their love for each other over and over in a tent by the lake.

"You're getting bugs all over it."

"You could drive yourself to the airport," my dad said. "And you could pay for two months' worth of parking fees too. Is that what you want?"

"I could just work at the diner again and not go at all," I said.

"You don't have a choice," he reminded me. "You're going."

For my sixteenth birthday, my parents gave me a used truck they bought off of a used-to-be-farmer from the Plains. It was yellow like egg yolk but sturdy. I liked that. They spent a good amount of money to make sure nothing was wrong with it, mechanically, but I was so afraid of everything by the time I turned sixteen that driving a "screechy, metal death-trap" wasn't among any of my desires. I was convinced that a car accident was the only way I *could* die, since killing myself on purpose took way too much courage. I slowly got over the fear of driving, but in the two years since I got it, I only drove my little yellow truck when I absolutely needed to and chose to walk almost everywhere else. There was no way I was going to drive it all the way to the airport.

My dad tried several times to teach me how to take care of it and how to do things like change the oil or check the tires for damage, but I was never going to learn that either. There was a lot that my dad tried to teach me, but the lessons I learned were not the lessons he intended. Lessons like keeping my mouth shut about politics, not out of respect for his opinion but out of respect for my own. Another lesson he taught me was that blame can shift to whomever and whenever if your voice is loud enough.

My dad wiped his hands on the sides of his pants and said, "Besides, you'll make more money than you do here, and you still have a laptop to pay off." Oh right, that goddamn laptop.

My dad was right about the money, though. At the time, I had no concept of money, really, and that led to a lot of sideways conversations. During the previous summer, I took a job as a waiter at the diner downtown earning just enough to pay for my gas (the only thing I was expected to pay for) and little else. By the end of the summer, I had spent so much of my earnings on timewasters that there wasn't much to say about my bank account. I wanted to work at the diner, though, because Kelly did, and Kelly was my best friend; we had enough in common like that. When I told Kelly that my cousin from California called, offering me a place to stay for the summer, she was right to ask, "You have a cousin in California!?"

I had an aunt in California, too, but I only ever told Kelly as little of the truth as possible. Once, I told her too much about a guy I liked, and she later asked about him in front of my parents. She didn't realize the harm in it, but I had to lie and say it was all a joke. Thank God they believed me and didn't make a big deal about it. Later, I told the same lie to Kelly and made sure to never tell her the whole truth again – even if she was my best friend.

At the airport, my mom gave me a long hug while my dad yanked my suitcase from the back of the car. She kissed my forehead like when I was a child, and that pulled the tears out from behind my eyes. I'm sure she thought she could hide hers back there too, but we were both wrong.

"Let us know when you get there," my dad said, hands in his pockets and his eyes at the pair of flight attendants walking in front of us.

"And don't forget about Kelly," my mom added, wiping her damp cheek with the inside of her wrist. "She seemed really excited about the whole pen-pal thing. Did you get paper?"

"Yeah, it's in my bag," I replied, teeth chattering. "With my ticket."

My dad said, "Good, don't lose it," and put his hand on my shoulder. "Love you son. Fly safe."

After my parents drove off, waving from the windows of their muddy car, I drifted aimlessly through the airport dragging my suitcase behind me. Airports are hellscapes for first-time fliers who lacked direction and didn't want to go anywhere anyway, but I found my way through it. I weaved through the ropes and metal detectors of bag check and security before finding my seat at the gate where I quickly put my earbuds in and drowned out the sounds of the airport. All I could think to do at that point was listen to music too loudly and ignore my mind's wanderings, but my phone buzzed in the pocket of my hoodie – the one I wore everywhere. It was a text.

(Alli)   Hey! Can't wait to see ya!
           Hot dogs for lunch?

I did miss Alli, honestly. Though she was my cousin, she was my first *actual* friend and one of the few people who saw me for who I was; no one before her could do that. She sent a letter in the mail a few years ago to reach out against the odds placed on displaced cousins caught in the middle of conflict. In the letter, she wrote about the time we dared each other to each eat a cricket, and how I was the only one to follow through. We used to be wild children who ran through fields and weedy lots and were thankful for sunsets or whatever fragments of our imaginations we still had. I would have been happier to see her, I think, if I wasn't so displaced in my own mind.

In one smooth motion, I turned my phone on its side and slid the top part up, revealing the small keyboard underneath. I only had the phone a year, but most of the letters and numbers had already worn off, leaving bare buttons behind. I knew where all the letters were, though, just not the numbers.

(Me)   sure sounds fine
(Alli)   Cool!
           Have a safe flight!
(Me)   thanks :)

I closed my phone just as smoothly as I opened it and slid it into the top-zipper section of my backpack before digging around for a sheet of paper to write my first letter to Kelly on. I figured that since I'd be in California for nine weeks, four sheets would be enough to give Kelly time to reply. Four sheets. Nine weeks. God, nine weeks of time wasted in Cali-fucking-fornia. I stared down at the pelicans and starfish printed into the flesh of the paper. I chose it because it reminded me of the aquarium and not because it showed some dock on the Pacific. I couldn't write anything more than "Hey Kelly," so I returned the paper to its place between my notebook and laptop.

When we finally started boarding, I didn't bother taking my earbuds out. I followed the people in front of me down the suspended hallway and into the belly of the vessel – all of us soon to be flung westward. So that I would feel more comfortable, my dad used his rewards points to pay for a business class ticket. But from what I could tell, the only difference between coach and business class was the leg room, but the people sitting by the emergency exits (which seemed like too much responsibility for anyone in sweatpants) had plenty of it. Every chair was upholstered in the same sticky fabric, and eighteen-year-olds were denied alcohol regardless of where they sat. I put my forehead against the window and watched as the fields below us were swallowed whole by the steel clouds. We flew away from the sun, toward America's promised land.

* * *

Since I only knew them when I was a child, there was very little I understood about the true nature of my dad's side of the family. One thing I noticed in all Marlows, though, was an obsession with being more than on time. The Marlows were the type of people to show up *way* too early for everything; it was in their blood. So, when I finally got to the pickup area of the San Diego airport, I was not surprised at all to see Alli standing at the front of the crowd with coffee and two breakfast burritos.

"Over here!" she called, smiling. Her aviator sunglasses glinted, framed by two brunette waves that fell amply past her shoulders. The rest was pulled back into a ponytail that sat just above the collar of her red leather bomber jacket. Though she was older now, Alli looked the way she always had – made of fire. And if her eyes weren't made green like mine, I'm sure they would have been carmine.

"It's so good to see you again," I said, which was the truth. I dropped my backpack at my feet and embraced my cousin in a full, heartfelt testimony.

"Even in boots, I'm *still* shorter than you!" she joked.

"Not by much!"

"Here." She held out a burrito wrapped in tin foil. Surely, she woke up early enough to make it herself.

"I'm good," I said. "I'm not that hungry."

"Take it, Ian." When she first told us that she was going to college for psychology, we knew that there was nothing better for someone as observant as Alli. And even though she dropped out, she was as keen as ever, so I grudgingly took the burrito.

We ate and talked about only the small things – like TV shows and road trips – while we waited for my suitcase at baggage claim. People came and went from the carousel, but I was not one of them. My brand-new teal suitcase did not emerge. Alli and I were not alone in this, as a small handful of others were also watching the same two suitcases slowly revolve around the track.

"I'm going to ask someone," Alli said, and decidedly turned toward the customer service counter. Away from her context, I went to the bathroom and made myself throw up in one of the stalls. I flushed away the breakfast burrito Alli gave me and wiped my face with toilet paper. That was my first time throwing up in California. It felt no different than throwing up in Colorado.

After washing my hands with the fluorescent pink soap, I chose a peppermint from the candy medley in my pocket and proudly tossed it into my mouth. I almost always carried candy with me, and peppermints were my favorite. Whether it was made of real sugar or not, candy was a great comfort to me.

On my way to rejoin Alli, I accidentally let the bathroom door slam behind me. It wasn't that I was careless, necessarily, but there was too much to think about by the time I thought to catch the door. Alli was alone at the carousel again, and I noticed that the smaller of the two suitcases had been claimed, and the solo-orbiter wasn't mine. I lined up my shoulders with Alli's.

"What'd they say?"

"Did you pack any extra clothes?"

"What? Why would they ask that?"

She pointed down at my backpack. "In there. Did you put any extra clothes in it? I guess some bags were put on the wrong plane, so they have to call us in a few days when they get here."

"Um, just a couple shirts," I replied, thankful that I chose to wear my nice jeans for the flight and not the gym shorts my mom recommended.

Alli said, "Well, let's go get you some clothes then," pushed her aviators further back on her face, and led me out into the West Coast wilderness.

3

Glass, stucco and vine – the three things that made up Alli's single story home in North Park. The bright, colorless walls were tethered to the ground only by the green and floral vines that held them. Windows filled the empty spaces, though the spotless windows were more like mirrors that reflected the neighborhood and the clouds and palm trees scattered around it. Contrails outlined the atmosphere above while we walked the searing sidewalk.

Inside her home was a testament to Alli's own fervidity – sleek and refined but not without a sharp edge. The walls and floors were smooth and cool-toned, while the furniture all seemed to be cut and forged from the same molten obsidian. Air, clean and crisp, filled my lungs, and I breathed it in fully. It was great to be out of the heat.

Alli set her keys down in the knotted wooden bowl on top of the glass coffee table. It reminded me of the wooden bowl my mom had on display in the kitchen but never used more than twice. I thought it was strange that two people who were so unlike each other had a similar taste in bowls.

On the coffee table were two books, but I only noticed them because of their oversized nature. *Film and Lens* was the larger of the two and slanted on top of it was Leo Tolstoy's *Anna Karenina*. My eyes drifted away from the books and toward the large cabinet bolted to the wall above the couch. Bottles of Alli's homemade tequila sat layered inside. What started as a small hobby blossomed into a little more than that as Alli obsessed over creating the perfect ratio of all-natural ingredients just to create the most intense-but-palatable distillation.

"Here's for the shower," Alli said, handing me a heap of plush, gray towels and an unopened bar of lavender soap. She pointed past the open-concept kitchen and said, "Your room is down the hallway. Let me know if you need any extra pillows or anything. Lunch is in an hour 'kay?"

"We just ate at the airport," I said, accepting the lavender heap.

"Oh yah. Hot dogs tomorrow, then, and we'll just eat at the restaurant."

"Wait, we're going there tonight?"

"*Yes* tonight! I thought you'd want to see it before you start tomorrow."

I said, "Okay, yah, sounds good," and turned down the hallway to where I would be living for the next two months.

Down the length of the hallway were two shelves that held a collection of knickknacks and books that meant more to Alli than I cared to ask about. There was a section of the bottom shelf dedicated to the Titanic and another portion slotted with dictionaries. Some of the dictionaries were written in English only, some were a showcase of translations between English and another language, and a handful were in Italian and Japanese. Of all things for Alli to collect, I thought dictionaries were obscure.

I opened the door to Alli's guest bedroom and took in the amber glow. The room smelled like oranges and spice, which paired well, I thought, with the lavender soap near my chin. A matching mahogany dresser and bed sat against the furthest wall, and a large, floor-length mirror stood to the left of the closet. Aside from the skylight above the bed, the light in the room came from the lamp in the corner.

I set the two bags of new clothes down by the dresser, then threw my backpack haphazardly onto the red and gray comforter on the bed. Without any care at all, I pulled the paper out of my backpack and put it in a sloppy stack on the dresser so that I could remember to write something down after the shower. I took the soap and towels to the bathroom with me and turned the hot water on high.

Steam filled the small space as I sat on the floor of the tub. My stomach growled, but I ignored it like usual and focused on my hands instead – two hands that used to hold small things like leaves and paper shreds. They slowly formed ridges and wrinkles from the water. I thought they looked too big, and I wasn't ready to hold such heavy things.

Bringing my knees to my chest and wrapping my arms around them, I rested my forehead in their valley. The water ran cool, and I thought it felt like rain. The rain meant a lot to me.

"Ian, let's go!" Alli called from the other side of the door, interrupting the rain. "You've been in there for almost an hour!"

"Okay!" I hollered back. With a sharp twist of the handle, I turned off the water and the rain was gone. I stood up slowly, shook the water from my hair, and wrapped the whole of my torso in the towel.

Back in my room, the air was cool against my damp skin. I dropped the towel and reached for the shirt on my bed, but I saw myself in the mirror, which was something that always made me stop. The sun poured in from the sunroof in a single beam that draped over my naked body – the same naked body I had been battling with for two years. As was my routine, I moved around erratically and viewed my body at every possible angle.

I hated what I was. My chest lacked definition and blended seamlessly into my abdomen. I pressed my flat hand against my lower gut, flexed, then turned again to prove to myself that I hadn't gained any weight since the last time I was in the mirror. I fixated on the hairs on my legs, wondering why the hell it didn't grow on the nickel-sized bald spot behind my right calf. Positions and postures. Left arm versus my right in terms of size and stature. Condemning eyes, which were too green for their own good, surveyed the bends and dips of my flesh. Imposing crests formed by whatever was beneath the fabric of my skin were sprawled out for lack of trying. Forward-facing feet, hips, clavicle. A lower back creeped up my spine and wrapped around my neck. All of that breath, pulse, and beat for a determined lacework of nerves and veins? I didn't see a reason for any of it.

Dirty blond hair. Dirty blond thoughts. Dirty blond existence.

"Ian!"

"Almost ready!" I called from my room while hurling my body into socks, shoes, jeans, shirt, and hoodie. I fixed my hair and grabbed my phone, ID, and debit card. I didn't carry a wallet, but it wouldn't have saved me any time if I had. Alli was waiting by the door by the time I emerged from the hallway. Her keys slammed against each other as she swung her lanyard back and forth like a metronome.

"Thanks for waiting," I said.

She cocked one of her eyebrows, then replied with a long, sarcastic "mmmhhm" and handed me a Chicago souvenir keychain. On it was a newly cut key to Alli's home. "I'm getting a number pad next month," she told me. "In the meantime, you'll use the key, so don't leave it anywhere."

I said, "All right, thanks," and followed Alli out of the glass, stucco and vine.

* * *

"Why do they call it Orange?" I asked, as we drove downtown from North Park. I was reading the bumper sticker off the car in front of us that read *Found in Orange County.*

"I think they used to grow a lot of oranges there," Alli replied. "It's only a few hours away if you want to go sometime." Maybe San Diego could have been known for growing oranges too, but all I saw were palm trees and rosewoods.

"Anything specific you want to do while you're here?" she asked me, adjusting the mirror to get the sun out of the way. She was focused on the road as she swerved in and out of highway lanes. Alli was a lead foot in both driving and conversation.

"Survive," I said.

As we drove, Alli made sure to point out landmarks and street names where local legends found themselves. Piecing together song references and scenes from movies could never have provided any true understanding of what it feels like to witness firsthand the gold and granite that was California. I could tell right away that San Diego was special. There was an authenticity there, a heart, determined to keep the pulse going.

"Here we go," Alli said, thrilled to have finally found an empty space in the parking lot behind the clustered buildings. She was right in saying it was a good idea for me to see the restaurant before my first shift. If I'm being honest, I was nervous about it. She said, "We usually come in through the patio since it's near the parking lot, but we'll go around the front so you can see it." The world is beautiful when the sun sets down on it and being out in San Diego at sunset had suddenly filled me with strange, irrational optimism for the summer and whatever it wanted with me.

We walked along the wooden fence of the patio while the tang of burnt kerosine mingled in the air with spices and prattled voices. The cement walkway led us past the patio and down between the restaurant and the neighboring building. Both brick walls of the two buildings were painted a glossy black and adorned with the brilliant glow of at least a hundred neon signs. It was beautiful. I turned my hands in their own shadows and watched my fingers drift in and out of the light.

Alli didn't even bother looking up as she glided through the narrow, neon passage.

She walked fast, always had, but I knew to keep up. We reached the end of the neon alley and turned left onto the busy downtown sidewalk where I was greeted by the glorious front of the restaurant which seemed to be carved out of wood. It was a total facade, but I thought it was gorgeous anyway. Intricate, golden Polynesian patterns stood out against the Saxe blue paint behind it. Small fire blazed in the torches that lined the entrance way while their flames danced on the surface of the koi pond.

"We're trying to get five stars," Alli told me. "It used to be three, but the owners did some renovations last year that got us another. Things like the fence, the koi pond, and that." She pointed up to the large, hand carved sign above the door. The wood was a perfect blend of sanded down splinters and paint. Parts of it were smooth, while the intentional cracks helped create the lettering.

"The Gilded Naupaka," I read out loud. "So, it's like a tiki bar?"

"It's better than a tiki bar, Ian, get a grip. It's a real nice place."

The front door swung open to reveal a tall, silver-blonde woman who emitted nothing short of grace and poise. She wore a knee-length skirt and a black button up shirt with silver buttons that caught the firelight. The sleeves of her shirt billowed out in sleek, flowing ruffles and her high heels seemed to carve into the pavement with each step she took toward us. Immediately, I could tell that there was a kindness about her. Alli lit up when she saw her, and I found that I, too, was beaming.

"Hey Yaryna!" Alli's bright words filled the space, making the koi dance. "Any patio spots left?"

"It is almost 6:30, what do you think?" Yaryna laughed. She had a glossy, Eastern European accent. Later, Alli told me that Yaryna moved to San Diego from Ukraine in order to escape the love of her father. Yaryna winked at us. "I think I can fit you back there. Just two?"

"Yep! Oh, this is Ian," Alli went on. "He's gonna be working with us for the summer."

"Oh?" Yaryna shifted her gaze to me. "How so far is California?"

"It's fine," I said.

Yaryna waited a moment, hoping I would say more, but I already said all I could about it. "Hm." Yaryna squinted. "It will grow on you."

Alli smirked at me, knowing that Yaryna saw through my attempt to hide whatever strange mix of frustration and excitement I felt. That's how Yaryna was, though. She saw how things were.

On our way to the patio, we had to cut through the main dining room, which was much larger than it appeared to be from the outside. Like so many of my perceptions, I was in a bigger world to navigate. My breathing was quick and shallow, as I imagined myself carrying large trays stacked with food through the winding aisles. I stirred in moment and tried to let my mind take it all in. The music, the rhythm, the forever moving vigor of the restaurant were monuments to me, and the small, Colorado diner in my mind was swallowed whole.

"I'm so glad your parents let you come out here," Alli said as we followed Yaryna.

"They made me, after they heard how much money you make."

I looked behind me as a door, hidden between ferns and fruit, slowly opened. I remember now how cinematic it was to watch the man who came out of the door carry three drinks in one hand and two in the other. He didn't let even a drop land outside of the glass. I'm sure he knew exactly what he was doing, and not spilling drinks was only one of the ordinarily amazing talents he had. I loved the way he walked like his feet had never, even once, betrayed him into falling. But even if he were to fall, the ground would surely rise to catch him because he was just that weightless. I was not the only one caught up in watching him. He was enthralling, and everyone knew it. There I was, just standing there in the middle of the restaurant watching a waiter carry drinks to a table. And though I didn't know it yet, I would soon love that unwitting king of California.

"Ian!"

I shook my head and caught up to Alli while the drinks and the music kept pulsing on the other side of the restaurant.

There was a fish tank next to the patio door with all types of tropical swimmers coasting back and forth between the coral. On the other side of the sliding door was the patio – a cement oasis of tiki lights, glass tables, and another koi pond. Stretched across the center of the patio was the bar and the large awning that covered it (not so that rain would miss it, but so that the bartender could stay out of the sun).

"That's where I'll be, mostly," Alli said, pointing to the bar.

Yaryna led us to a small table positioned against the fence. Aside from the lights behind the bar, the many torches provided enough light to read our menus. I liked the occasional cracking sounds they made.

On the cover of the menu was a pencil-sketched image of a flower tucked neatly in the folds of a large, ornate leaf. It only had half of its petals, though, like someone had plucked off the other four.

"That's a Naupaka," Alli said, not lifting her eyes from the menu. I tilted my head.

"Huh?"

"The flower." She tapped on the menu with her ruby red nail. "It's what the restaurant is named after."

"Why a flower?" I asked, not that I had any issue with it being a flower. I was just curious. Alli took a long sip of her drink, then set it down neatly.

"It's a cool story, actually," she said. "It's about a beautiful princess, Naupaka, and the man she fell in love with. They were from different worlds since she was a princess and the sister of gods, and he was, well, nowhere close to that. Pele, Naupaka's sister, was jealous and forced her lover up the mountain. Then she sent Naupaka down to the sea. Her other sisters, who were also gods but nicer than Pele, turned them each into flowers. That's why this type of flower only grows near the shore or on the mountain. If you hold two of them together, they complete each other."

I stared back at Alli. The story was beautiful, and I was totally engaged, honestly, but she must have thought I wasn't listening.

"Andrew tells it *way* better. Anyway, it's cool too because the owners, who are married, can't always be together since his wife flew back a couple years ago to help her mom. They make trips back and forth between their families and the restaurant, but not always at the same time. The restaurant shows how they are two halves of the same flower."

"Oh, neat," I said, nodding. Then, as if only a name was enough to justify a question I asked, "Andrew?"

"Yeah, Andrew. He's great, you'll love him."

4

I only slept four hours that night, but that wasn't too different from most nights. It didn't matter what time I went to bed, falling asleep quickly was always impossible.

When I was ten years old, I mourned the death of my parents. Neither of them really died, but I woke up nightly, sobbing, because in my nightmares they had. This is where, I think, my fear of losing people came from. I was convinced that anything and everything could rip my parents away from me.

My mom quit her job so she could stay home and raise me in my early years while my dad worked. At the time, my mom's side of the family was the only side that was ultimately unreachable. She ran off with my dad when she was only seventeen and severed all connection to her lineage. This made her sad – rightly so – and she cried every time she talked about them. And every time she cried, I was there to comfort her. I was my mother's consoler.

"Burned bridges," my dad said, matter of fact, but he didn't handle emotions well, like he was afraid of them. I realize that now. He wouldn't speak about his dead father, but slammed doors as he used them – the fridge, the bedroom, the front door leading up from the sidewalk.

Slamming doors and crying mothers made their way into my nightmares, and soon after, my parents started dying. I woke up sobbing almost every night, which was a lot for a ten-year-old. And of course, I couldn't tell my parents why I was crying so much in my sleep because it would only make them more concerned – more slammed doors and more tears. Alone in my room, I breathed through it, staring at the void on the ceiling, and told myself it wasn't real. Rationalizing led to overthinking until I passed out, but when the next day got over with, I was afraid to sleep. After a year, the nightmares disappeared and the insomnia I developed settled in.

I had a lot to think about during my first night in California. Most of my thoughts consisted of frustrations like *I hate how hot this room is* and self-imposing questions like *why do I complain so much?* In reality, I think I was mostly just nervous to meet everyone. Three hours of lying awake on the firm bed in Alli's guest room led to waking up at 7 a.m. with only four hours of sleep to rely on.

Alli and I got to the restaurant at nine in the morning so that I had an hour or so to fill out paperwork and ask Carol any questions before my shift officially started.

Carol was the assistant manager, but her "kind-yet-assertive" demeanor allowed her to act with more power than that. She was in on it with the owners and was left in charge of everything when they weren't around to call the shots. By the time she had her way, the only thing that she had no control over was the schedule, but Carol didn't seem diplomatic enough to organize people's lives, and even may have appreciated that Alli made the schedule.

Yes, Carol liked being in charge of things, but there was also an exceptional warmth and friendliness about her that made you feel like nothing was ever the matter. She was stout and stalwart, with red hair and a nebula of freckles that spanned across her nose and up her brow. Proud of her deep Wisconsin roots, Carol seemed to think that working in Southern California was an act of survival, and so she was one of those people who unintentionally cut people off in conversation.

"So, whatcha think of California?" she said. Her voice was very loud.

"It's fine so far," I said. "But I thought there would be less traffic and–"

Carol scoffed. "Traffic's a way of life, kid, get used to it!" I smirked and followed her out of the office. After a brief tour of the restaurant, kitchen, seating sections and break room, she pulled a clipboard from off the host stand and used a dry erase marker to write my short name on a section of the restaurant's floor plan. "Alli put you on the patio today?"

"That's fine!" I said in a forced enthusiasm. Alli told me earlier that morning that she intentionally put me on the patio because it was closest to the bar, and she could help me if I needed her to. Of course, I thought I would be fine since I spent all of last summer waiting tables at the diner. That was in Colorado, though, where I didn't have to worry about more than two tables at a time, so the very frustrating and fast-paced shift that soon followed at the Gilded Naupaka made me question all of my abilities.

Customer service was never something I struggled with, and I wasn't clumsy. It was the number of people that I failed to keep up with. The patio was the largest section, which also meant it had the largest group seating – *everyone* wanted to eat out there. Who would take the trip to San Diego and not sit outside?

The massive trays of food were, as I assumed, a nightmare to port from the kitchen to the patio, but I didn't drop any food. Not once. I did bump into things, though, including other servers. They were patient with me, thank God, but I knew it bothered them – it would bother me too. One time, I accidentally backed into the fish tank. Patrick, the lead host, saw and blithely joked, "Dude, you're running into things I forgot we had!"

I laughed it off since I was only somewhat in my element and certainly not in the right frame of mind to say anything about it. Despite how hard I tried to stay on top of everything, I fell behind. Other servers offered to help me, but I threw back careless things like, "I'm fine, thanks," and "No, I got it." Then, shortly after 1 p.m., Pat started giving tables from my section to other servers. I understood why, but I still hated it. Alli noticed.

"Ian!" she called from behind the bar, setting two cool drinks down on the granite. "You good?" she asked.

"Yah, why?"

"Because that's the fourth table you lost this hour." I turned and saw Chris taking the appetizer order for table twenty-six – *another* table given away to *another* server.

"Oh, yeah, I told him he could have it."

Alli saw right through my impulse. "You know this is a city, right? You're gonna need to pick up the pace. How much have you made?"

I sighed, reached into the front pocket of my apron, and pulled out a sorry collection of bills. "Like, fifty bucks."

Alli shook her head and picked the drinks up off the bar. I watched over my shoulder as she set them down at table sixteen. She put her hand on the customer's chair and used her other hand to point to something past the fence. The group at the table let out a wild laugh as she drifted back to me, her neophyte cousin, still hunched at the bar. "Andrew will be here soon," she said. "I'm putting him in your section."

"I don't want any help, Alli, I can figu–"

"No, you need it. Also, he's really good and can show you how to get these people to blow a hundred on drinks alone."

* * *

Rain – the lung cleanser and softener of scars. It flooded the caverns of my inner ear while I tried to count.

One. One, two, th- one…. two, three…one, two

Calling the number of raindrops out loud didn't help, so I tried to count breaths instead. I only got to fourteen. The rain was too loud, and I had a hard time focusing on the rise and fall of my ribs. But when the rain came and rinsed the sidewalk in a confluent surge, I realized that killing myself wasn't something I was strong enough to see the end of, so I put my forehead to the pavement instead.

Spring rain pooled in the basin of my bare lower back before spilling out over the slopes of my waistline. I had nothing but gym shorts on. A free body. Clavicle, elbows, chin, knees, talus …points of contact pressed into the sidewalk while I attempted to count the raindrops again. They splashed against the tops of my ears where I could feel them the most. Almost rhythmically. Almost individually. Coarse Colorado rain helped me find myself again and reminded me that I'm not my feet or my name. I was myself, but still let myself disintegrate into miry pieces. All at once, I was existing for no one and let my tears join the raindrops as they purged my restless mind.

The rain saved my life that night, but that rain, regardless of what I owed to it, was nothing compared to meeting Andrew.

"So, this is the cricket-eater, huh?"

At once, my memory of lying in the rain was gone. His voice was smooth and unbroken, which conveyed a boundless self-assurance that could never be confused with arrogance. Andrew was entirely sincere and knew exactly who he was. That's all there was to it. And it was everything I noticed about him the night before, when I watched him, the king of California, bring drinks to a crowded table.

There were a lot of things about myself that I avoided out of fear, but the one I was most afraid of was how I felt around beautiful men like Andrew. His hair was wavy and dark with one side held behind his ear. The sun lived in his skin, and when his kind, brown eyes met mine, I inhaled sharply through my nose. My face was warm and my eyes were dodging around. I folded my thoughts in on themselves so that they couldn't get anywhere near my tongue. As painful as it was to reduce myself to nothing, I was sure it hurt less than the alternative.

"I have no idea what you're talking about," I snapped, throwing a glare at Alli. She returned it with a shrug, and Andrew's face fell. I knew he was just trying to break the ice, and I met it with, well, more ice. I said, "Are we done here?" and shoved my way between Alli and Andrew before either of them could say anything.

The hours – *hours* – that followed were filled with nothing but awkward exchanges between Andrew and me. We went opposite ways through doors, often trading strange glances. He tried a couple of times to talk to me, to offer his help to someone so lost in it all like I was, but I ignored him until he finally yielded. Alli pulled me to the side and told me how rude I was being, but hell, I ignored her too. There was nothing she could say about it that would keep me from my safeguard.

Then, toward the end of the shift, after I lit the last of the torches, Andrew and I met again at the patio door. I stepped to the side, allowing him to move on, but he didn't. He just stood there, calm and cool with his arms crossed. His eyes were fixed on mine, and his whole face was held with impassive control.

"Are you going to move?" I asked. Andrew slowly shook his head, so I shifted my position to match his – arms crossed and all. "Well, I need in there."

A small smirk formed on the left side corner of his mouth as he uncrossed his arms and revealed a single, fresh-cut lemon wedge. As if it was some ceremonial effort, Andrew set the lemon wedge on the top of my head, whispered "Lemon," then sailed past me. I stood there in disbelief with a cold, wet wedge of citrus on my head.

He called me *Lemon*.

5

"That was great, thanks Alli!" said Kayla as she set her knife and fork down on the plate. She was engaged to a guy from Seattle who lived in an apartment downtown, but Kayla spent a great deal of time eating and drinking at Alli's place. Dillan, Kayla's fiancé, proposed to her the year before by surprising her with a large stone and an Alaskan cruise, but Kayla could only talk about the wedding planned for later that summer. It was Kayla's third night over since I got there, and I was amused by the eclecticist.

"No problem," Alli replied, adding Kayla's plate to the stack.

"You and Ian need to come over. I make the *best* sukiyaki! It's even better than my mom's, which is saying a lot."

"It'd be fun," Alli said.

"Wouldn't it?" Kayla went on. "We could go swimming, play dumb games, read palms...all of it."

Alli winked at me. "Kayla's a fortune teller."

"No one can tell the future." Kayla's voice was sharp and quick, like she was offended but couldn't mention it. "But I can do a quick reading for you, if you want." I realized, then, that she was talking to me. "Here, hold on." She reached behind her to the jacket she draped over the chair before dinner and pulled out a satin-wrapped block from one of the side pockets. It was a deck of tarot cards.

After moving the two, identical sections of her jet-black center part to behind her ears, Kayla pointed her blue eyeliner at me and let the words "Are you ready?" fall from her thin lips.

Even though my parents were each raised in religious households, neither of them claimed to be religious since becoming adults. They believed that everything they had in life, all of the wonderful things about themselves that they never had to once question, was not by design but rather by their own hands. So, I wasn't religious either. I didn't believe in anything other than my own experiences, which I depended on above all else. Regardless of whatever Kayla thought the deck of cards could tell me, I knew it was going to be nothing more than that – an experience.

"How does it work?" I asked coyly, not wanting to seem too interested.

Kayla handed me the cards. "Move them around, look at them if you want, and then hand them back."

I randomly shuffled through the cards. They were designed in a gorgeous and intricate 1920s influence.

The backs of the cards were coated in a deep, rich navy blue kept behind gold accents that caught the light only to scatter it again. On the front, the artistic style was consistent, but each individual scene was unique. One showed a burly, mustached bartender positioned over five martini glasses; three of which were toppled and spilling over the counter. Another showed a stunning woman in a short dress beneath a large star. She was intentionally emptying bottles of wine into what looked like a pool of rainwater. In the same reflective gold as the back, the Roman numeral XVII was embossed on the bottom-left corner of the card. I put the card back in with the others, smoothed the deck, and handed the stack back to Kayla.

"So, is there anything specific you want to ask?" she said, shuffling the cards. I liked the sound of her long nails against them.

"Not really," I said. "Whatever I need to know about, I guess."

She squinted, pursing her lips like she was trying to evaluate my sincerity. "Let's just start with one card, then."

Kayla looked up into the ceiling and beyond into what I assumed were the cosmos she imagined above us. In front of her, her hands carefully sorted and mixed the cards before finally fanning out the deck, face down, and selecting a single card from the sea of navy and gold.

"Aahhh," Kayla sighed. "Number seven. The Chariot." She flipped the card on its back and slid it my way for me to pick up. The scene portrayed an assertively dressed character in a suit, poised in the driver seat of a LaSalle. The car was vertically divided into two colors. A stark white coated the left, jet black made up the right, and only the headlights were identical. The driver was off to some unknown world across a bridge while the sun set behind them. And just like the other cards in the deck, there were golden Roman numerals on the lower left corner. VII.

"Chariot?" I asked. "Is it good or bad?"

"None of the cards are good or bad. It all has to do with what it means to *you*." She waited a moment, then, "Does anything on it stand out to you?"

I stared into the cardstock, trying to pluck out from the details anything that, as Kayla described, "stood out." It all seemed so standard to me, though, and at first, I didn't see anything paramount. Sure, the art was pretty, but pretty doesn't mean prophetic. To me, it was just a picture printed on a pretty card.

But as I was about to hand the card back to Kayla, a small bauble impressed me. Pinned to the driver's suit coat was a silver-beaded lobster brooch, shining in the light of some imaginary art deco sun.

"The lobster."

"The lobster?" Kayla repeated, sweeping some crumbs off her lap. I turned the card to face her and pointed at the brooch, but she couldn't see it, so I shrugged and passed it to her.

"Ohhh." She paused, inspecting the tiny detail of the card. It must have been hard, I think, for someone who considered herself an expert to not have an answer right away. I watched her fixate on the lobster too, trying to make it mean something. "Maybe the artist just liked lobsters, so they put one in the picture. It doesn't mean anything, just part of the artwork."

"So... what does the card mean, then?"

She glanced up at me and remembered again why she was holding the card in the first place. "Well, you can look at it a couple of different ways. Usually, it represents overcoming challenges, like maybe a long day at work, or maybe-"

"Or maybe you have to deal with this bullshit!" Alli hollered from the kitchen followed by a wild laugh. Kayla flipped her off, without turning, but the smirk she had told me she enjoyed the banter. Alli's blatant criticism was a compliment to Kayla's accept-all personality.

"Anyways," Kayla continued, "it means that you need more balance in your life. Like, look at the car." She got up and glided over to me. The long sleeves of her shirt billowed at her sides. "The driver is going one direction, but if they turned even just a little to left or right, the car would go off the bridge...where do you feel like you lack balance?"

I glanced up at her. This was a question I knew the answer to but wasn't expecting to answer out loud in the middle of my cousin's dining room. The words would get all caught up in each other on the table for everyone to see, illuminated by the light of Edison bulbs and follow-up questions. No, I didn't say anything about it. Instead, I said, "I don't know," and left it at that.

"Maybe that's why the card came up for you, then."

I stared dully at the card in Kayla's hand while Alli came in from the kitchen. "Ian doesn't believe in this shit."

"If you want to take a pic of the card, you can," Kayla said, ignoring my obtrusive cousin. "So, you don't forget."

"It's ok," I replied, picturing the silver lobster brooch in my mind. "I'll remember."

* * *

I was stacking dishes when Alli called, "Hey! Ian!" from the living room where she and Kayla went with drinks to chat after dinner. Kayla brought over a half-empty bottle of vodka, but Alli insisted on the cocktail she came up with using her own tequila.

"What?" I hollered back, not letting the ceramic bowls clash against each other as I set them in the cabinet.

"Wanna take a drive with us?"

"Where would we go at ten at night?!"

"It's *barely* 9:40," she assured me. "And we're going to Andrew's. I guess he's having a small thing at his place tonight."

I said, "Have fun!" and grabbed another stack of ceramic dishes.

"He said you could come, too, if you wanted." The smirk on Kayla's face was almost sinister, which made me pause to consider the ulterior. Though it had been a few days, I was still not over the fact that someone as impressive as Andrew noticed how bitter I was and did something about. I mean, he called me Lemon. Something so sour, rarely sweet, and wrapped in a bitter peel.

I said, "I doubt that," and joined them in the living room.

"It's true! Despite your attitude, he still invited you. Amazing huh?" Though I didn't like to hear it, there was truth lodged somewhere in Alli's sarcasm. And as much as I was afraid of it, I did want to see him again

"Fine," I said. "I'll go." Alli nodded, Kayla smirked, and I groaned. Within twenty minutes, Alli, Kayla, and I were on our way to La Jolla.

Kelly, my best friend and unintentional spiller of secrets, had criticized me several times for never sneaking out. She used to say how lame it was that someone like me wouldn't even *try* to get out from under the rug every once in a while and join her and the other stray dogs as they climbed in and out of empty spaces swinging back bottles of stolen liquor into the guts of their gaping self-affluence. Once, she even went as far as explaining that teens with parents as demanding as mine were more likely to sneak out. Well, Kelly snuck out all the time, and from what I could tell, her mom was not demanding, let alone around. So maybe sneaking out was just part of Kelly's nature. Or maybe it wasn't, but she wished it was. It didn't matter. She snuck out, and I was always there to hear about her adventures.

I never thought I was missing out, especially when she dominated the conversation with details of run-ins with cops and what she called "reasons" to risk it all. These "reasons" were most often just other guys from our town, but now and then, someone from somewhere else would visit, and Kelly made it her mission to find what party he would be at.

I didn't have a "reason," so I stayed home at night, away from parties. And since I didn't ever sneak out to parties, the one at Andrew's was the first party I ever went to.

In the car, I struggled to focus and my teeth were chattering against each other like they do whenever I got nervous. Alli asked if I was cold, but I wasn't – I was sweating, actually. I reached for the temperature control and blasted cold air, which I'm sure Alli thought was strange for a person with chattering teeth to do.

The radio was blaring something raucous, which I hated, so I put in my earbuds and pressed shuffle on my budget mp3 player. I didn't want to listen to anything at all, but there was no way I was going to listen to Alli's music.

We went north on the Five to La Jolla. As we drove, we passed under countless streetlights that proudly towered over those of us on the road. Their light filled the car with momentary gleams that passed over my arm, up my shoulder, and across my face as if they were scanning to see how worthy I was to be there at all – to simply exist as I am under streetlights on the highway. I wondered if the streetlights detected how torn I felt, but even if they didn't, it was under their light that I found the way to describe the two disjointed halves of my being.

One half, made from a desire for intimacy and adventure, was drifting carelessly and free in the space above the city. The other half, made from actuality and self-loathing, was crammed down into the cracks in the asphalt joined by rust and tarmac. The light from the streetlights was unable to reach these places, so all that the city saw of me was my body: made of meat and marrow, hidden in clothing, and propped up against a car window.

Shortly after exiting the highway, Alli reached over, pulled out my earbud, and asked me to read her Andrew's address from her phone, which I did, but not before scowling. She started listing off street names under her breath.

"I've been here before," she said. "It just looks different at night." I believed her because her sense of direction was much better than mine. I was absolutely directionless. Alli threaded through the avenues until we pulled over in front of a small collection of apartments called *Casa Del Norte*. I was still sitting in the car looking up at the indiscernible shapes and bends of the building when Alli and Kayla were already halfway up the walkway. Kayla carried the half-empty bottle of vodka, sloshing it around as she swung her arms. There was a large number eight stuck to the wall next to the door. I got out of the car and joined the other two at the doorway where the shadowy silhouette of Andrew was waiting to greet us.

"Lemon! You came!"

I smirked, teeth still chattering, and gave a weak "yep."

Andrew forced a small laugh and stepped aside, welcoming us into his apartment. As I walked past him, I noticed the faint scent of sandalwood and pine, but it was quickly overtaken by the variety of other scents from the rapturous night.

The music was quick and heavy. Lights were sunken in on themselves, and voices were muddled while people swirled the ice around in their cups like oracles. Small crowds morphed and divided through some metropolitan mitosis, and the ones who danced were the lucky ones because they didn't need words or wages. They had their music and primal movements. Occasionally, a holler broke out above the speakers, calling others to join in on the pulse-beat electric.

I was trying to look back at Alli and Kayla when a hand landed on my shoulder. "What can I get you?"

I turned and was nose-to-nose with a friendly, red-cheeked man wearing a necklace/bracelet combo of no less than seventeen glow-sticks.

"What do you have?" I asked, fidgeting with the four pieces of candy in my pocket. The man closed one eye and looked up with the other, calculating. My phone buzzed, but I ignored it.

"Uhhhh, I can make a painkiller, I guess, since we got th–"

"Sounds great," I said. I didn't care what was in a "painkiller," and I still haven't looked it up. All I cared about was finding something to dull my perception, but I only took one sip of it before I poured it down the sink in the bathroom. On the left-side ledge of the sink was a bottle of cologne. I took the lid off and sniffed around the nozzle; it smelled just like Andrew. Without even thinking about it, I turned the nozzle toward the inside of my jacket and trapped a full draft of sandalwood and pine into its threads. Suddenly realizing the weight of what I did and the motivation behind it, I snapped the lid back on and returned it to its place on the sink. With an empty plastic cup, I left the bathroom. Too embarrassed to ask for a different drink, I threw the cup away in the kitchen trash.

Alli and Kayla were no longer at the party. I was told by someone in big, yellow glasses that in the short time I was in the bathroom, Alli, Kayla, and a few others left to get more alcohol. Annoyed and nervous, I weaved in and out of groups of people and made my way out onto the empty balcony.

The lights of San Diego cut through the night. My eyes followed the span of the glow and found the freeway we followed to Andrew's. I watched as veins of vehicles passed under streetlights and imagined myself as the passenger leaning against the car window. The moon was bright, even in comparison to the city lights, and it made my skin look pallid. I wasn't electric at all, just alone on a balcony at a party in La Jolla.

The door behind me slid open, but I didn't bother turning around because I was fixed on lights.

"You okay?" Andrew asked, confirming that I was no longer free to be alone on the moon-bleached balcony. "I'm fine, why?"

"Just checking." His sincerity was raw yet gritty, like unfiltered honey. "It's just...you seem–"

"I said I'm fine." He nodded and looked down at the balcony planks and I knew I needed to chill. "I'm sorry," I said. "I'm just out of it. I am happy to be here, though, I think, so thanks for the invite."

The mood lofted there for a while in the quiet until a car alarm went off down the block. A woman in flip-flops ran down to the car, fighting the air with her key fob. The alarm stopped. Silence went on.

"Do anything fun today?" he asked me.

"Oh, you know, just another day filled with fortune tellers," I joked. "You?"

"Same. Just can't fight 'em off this time of year. If someone tells a hundred fortunes by September, they win a bike." Andrew turned so that his back leaned against the wooden beam – the same beam that held my forearms – and we both calmed from the simper. "I'm glad you're here too." He pulled a joint and lighter out of his pocket. "I thought I fucked it up with the whole lemon thing." The end of the joint lit up in brilliant crimson then cooled again as he released a breath of smoke. It drifted up from his mouth before dissolving away.

"I deserved it," I said. "I was awful."

"Yes, you were," he replied laughing. "Here."

He passed the joint to me, and I accepted in humor. I might not have ever snuck out, but that didn't mean I didn't cause trouble in other ways. I was an expert at sneaking edibles out of my dad's nightstand from between his pills and porn. With bold breath, I inhaled and let the fullness of the night fill my lungs. I held it in even as I passed the joint back to Andrew. It burned, but I held it in only so I could exhale at the same time as Andrew and mix my smoke with his.

I took in his features while the lights of La Jolla framed the scriptures of his face in blue and white light. Daffodil cream from the light fixture behind me lit up the other parts of him and I was absolutely eclipsed.

"Andrew, get in here! We're waiting for ya!" an interrupting voice called from inside.

"Coming!" Andrew answered. I followed him to the living room where the crowd had merged to form one large city chorus that began to sing a beautifully broken *Happy Birthday.*

"It's your birthday!?" I asked as soon as the pulse of the party returned.

"Not until Wednesday. Hey, are you hungry?"

"What?"

"Let's go get something to eat." He walked through the crowded apartment like there wasn't a party at all. I looked over at the strange crowd then back at Andrew who was already at the front door.

Victim of impulse, I abandoned the party too.

6

Stray dogs – the people who run around neighborhoods at night with nothing to do but wander. People who were reckless, wild, and free for no other reason than because they wanted to be. They were feral people who had been liberated from prophecy through their esoteric conjecture and howled in the streets at each other instead of at the moon because stray dogs didn't know where the moon was most of the time. Stray dogs were hard to catch but easy to find because stray dogs were everywhere, and I would be lying if I said I didn't want to be one of them.

I got a taste of it, though, while Andrew and I wandered the sidewalks of La Jolla looking for a place to eat. It was almost midnight. I was surprised to hear crickets.

"Found one!" Andrew shouted, as he pointed to the fast-food place on the other side of the intersection. We raced each other through the crosswalk; dodging traffic and cursing the curb. I beat Andrew to the door, but it didn't matter. We were thrilled enough just by being in on it together.

"Oh, it's closed," I said, pointing to the sign taped to the door. Andrew squinted at the sign, which I thought took him too long if he were serious about reading it. I looked around us and thought everything felt brighter, louder, and faster. I didn't even notice that Andrew grabbed my hand before I was being led to the other side of the restaurant.

"What are w-"

"Only the inside's closed," he said. "The drive-through's open, though!" I stopped and let go of his hand. Andrew smiled and winked at me from over his shoulder while I stood there and watched the reigning king of California order two burgers right from the drive-through window. He had to stand on his toes to reach the window, and I thought it was a whole new type of endearing.

"Don't eat it yet," he said, handing me the warm sandwich wrapped in wax-coated paper. "I wanna show you something, kay?" I nodded. He led and I followed.

We didn't turn on the same street that he lived on. Instead, we turned down a street that led slightly away from his apartment, and after about fifteen minutes, we found ourselves standing on the lawn of a small house.

It was a single-story structure with dull, peeling paint, but even in the dark I could tell by Andrew's face that this house was more than that to him.

"I used to live here," he said, clearing his throat. "When I was a kid, my parents, uh, they couldn't afford it anymore. They sent me to my grandpa's." There was a calmness about Andrew, as recollection tugged at his brow. "He hit me. Not all the time, but hard enough to make me stay outta his fuckin' way. It didn't matter. So, one time I shoved back. He kicked me out."

Andrew turned and basked in the house and its pieces. He said, "This way" and led me to the back of the house where he then climbed the worn-out planks of the fence, just like he did as a child. He helped me secure my footing and pointed out where to grab the window, the pipe, and finally, the roof.

The world above the city was awash in a profuse stratos blue, which was not at all what I expected to find trespassing on the roofs of childhood homes. Hickory smoke rose from the backyard belonging to the pink stucco house a few doors down, and its inhabitants cheered each other on while they danced to slow music. An occasional airplane would glide over us while the tops of in-person palm trees peeked out over the neighborhood; I thought of reaching out to touch their fronds. *How is this real?* I thought, but that's just the kind of thing stray dogs found. It was more than lights, more than music, and more than anything I knew existed in the first place. It was unfiltered adolescence and it was alive.

Andrew saw it, too, I think, because he smiled when he saw how wide my green eyes were. I wondered how many times he must have climbed up there just to look out at the world – to escape the ground level of standard perspective and rise above it all.

For almost an hour, we stayed there high and happy to be sitting so close to each other. I was hugging my knees and he sat cross-legged while we talked about our families, our viewpoints, our histories. Everything. And we listened to each other, truly. He was interested in me and I was fascinated by his marvels. I wanted to hear all of whatever cosmic entities came together to make him the way he was.

I learned about his dad's parents, who came to California from Baracoa, Cuba, and how important it was to them that their son make a living however he could, as long as a living was made. And he did it, too, by painting peoples' houses and landscaping the ones that really needed it. His mom grew up in Placerville and worked at a hardware store that sold paint to single, house-painting men. They wanted a child. That's what they told him, at least, but they couldn't afford to raise one. Andrew's grandfather took him in when he was eight, and his parents moved back to Cuba. When Andrew turned fourteen, his grandfather started to beat him in hopes to prevent a homo from muddying the legacy. It was hard to listen to, but I could see how even at the age of sixteen, Andrew knew it was safer to sleep in strange places.

"So, you speak Spanish?" I asked him.

He said, "nope," in a short, matter-of-fact sort of way. "I wasn't taught."

"Do you want to learn?"

"Of course. It sucks not knowing your family's words for the things around you."

I nodded, and we went back to watching the world. After a while, I told him about how afraid I was of everything, even my own body, and how the last thing I wanted was to lose my parents since they were the only family I had until Alli reached out. Andrew asked me what I wanted to do with my life.

"No idea," I told him.

He replied with a quick "so what?" which made me laugh, I don't know why. I guess I appreciated hearing something so unconcerned. But since I had nothing else to say, I leaned over and pressed my lips into his; converging at our quasar. I was shaking, particularly in my supporting arm, but not from fear and not nerves either. All I could do about the excitement was close my eyes and let the night become sound only. Andrew's lips softened as he pressed back into me.

It was a short kiss that lasted for only a moment, but we each smirked as we exhaled back into the rooftop locale. I didn't need smoke to prove our breaths mixed because he said, "We just did that," and leaned onto the shingles.

"So what?" I replied and took a huge bite of burger. We didn't say much afterwards, but I know that he was just as happy as I was to be looking in the same direction as someone else for a change. I was young, I know that, but I *felt* young. That was the first bite of burger I kept down in a year, all because I kissed the king of California.

Back at Andrew's apartment, the once-electric party had reduced down to nothing but societal radio static. There were no more than four or six people milling about while music deluged the room in throbs. Every flat surface accessible was coated in empty cups, and even emptier thoughts clung to the inner minds of those passed out on the floor.

Alli was half awake, slouched and poised like a vintage advertisement for the bottle of gin in her hand. As soon as she noticed that Andrew and I had come back, Alli forced herself up. She had to catch herself on the back of the couch, which told me that her "thoroughly responsible" personality had been diluted in party drinks.

"Where the hell have you been?" she said, forcing her index finger into my sternum.

"Hey, you left too!" I protested.

"At least I TOLD you when I left!"

I tilted my head and squinted, which was my way of saying *no the fuck you didn't.* "Anyways, you, uhhhhh...we gotta go man," she went on. "Do you work tomorrow? I work tomorrow. Let's go." She stumbled between us while tossing her keys at me. They fell to the carpet in a bronzy *thud,* but she didn't notice.

"Hey, can I text you sometime?" Andrew asked me on my way out the door. He handed me his phone that was open to a blank message. All of the numbers on his phone were there, so I was glad we did it this way instead of using mine. After I sent the text, I felt my pocket buzz, letting me know that I had his number too, and that I made a little more than a friend out there in the wilds of California.

I said "goodnight" and he said, "Goodnight Lemon," which I liked. And on the whole way home, as my cousin slept with her forehead against the car window, I was happy, awake, and new. I let the streetlights scan me the whole way because there were no parts of myself that I could hide from anymore.

He called me Lemon...So what?

* * *

"You can't just *not* eat, Ian."

The fluorescent lights glared down on the mostly empty cafeteria. Metal clangor fell out of the kitchen while Mrs. Rhytner sat next to the shaky, teeth-chattery fourteen-year-old I used to be. Four minutes earlier, the large cafeteria was filled with voices of other teens who either ate their food or didn't. Mrs. Rhytner noticed that I was one of the ones who didn't.

Caring for kids like me was all Mrs. Rhytner did, but I just wanted her to shut up and leave me alone. It didn't matter how many questions she asked me or hypotheticals she offered; I was not going to give Mrs.

Rhytner a single reason for why I dumped my food into the trash can.

"Do we need to call someone?"

"No."

The cafeteria was loud, but my mind was louder. I stared down at the waxy floor, fixating on the trash and crumbs sprinkled over it. Disgusting.

Mrs. Rhytner said "Ian" like it was a question, but like hell I was going to answer. Defeated, she let me go to class only to have me called out again to chat with my parents. My mom and dad, of course, never would have understood, but at least Mrs. Rhytner's office was warmer than the cafeteria.

"How long has this been going on?" my mom asked.

I lied and said, "Not that long," and tried not to bounce my leg so much. That only made my chattering worse, though, because I wasn't that good of a liar yet.

"Since October," Mrs. Rhytner said.

"October?"

"I'm afraid so, Mr. Marlow."

My dad shook his head, huffed, and slumped back into the stiff chair across from Mrs. Rhytner's desk. In a voice that rang more stern than sad, my mom turned to me.

"Why haven't you been eating?"

"Not hungry."

My mom said, "You know we pay for those meals, right?" but I shrugged and rolled my eyes. She hated that. "So, we've been paying for thrown-away meals for *four months*, and you are this nonchalant!?"

I didn't answer. I stared wide-eyed and hollow at the red and yellow painting on the wall behind Mrs. Rhytner's desk. My mom's eyes bore into the side of my head, but not deep enough that thoughts could seep out.

"Thank you for bringing this to our attention," my mom said. She took a deep breath and stood up quickly; clutching her arms across her waist to prove her stoicism.

"Of course. If you need anything–"

My dad made his way to the door, confident that the conversation was over. "We'll talk with Ian, and you'll let us know if this happens again."

I stood up too and gave a quick glance over my shoulder to Mrs. Rhytner, who shook my mom's hand. I thought I saw her whisper something to my mom, but it wouldn't matter if she did. There was nothing she could have said that would have changed my mom's new perspective of me.

Instead of returning me to class, my parents excused me for the day, drove me to a fast-food restaurant and sat down with me at a booth near the window. Neither of them ordered food for themselves, but the number two combo – a burger and fries – sat on a tray in the middle of the table. My dad's firm hand gripped the sandwich and threw it down in front of me.

"Eat."

I picked up the burger and intentionally pressed my fingertips into the soft bun, causing it to break inward. It was warm, in all its global glory. My dad nodded in approval as my teeth sunk shyly into the side of the burger, and I only chewed a few times before swallowing the painful lump. I was humiliated – forced to swallow mouthfuls of shame like that. My mom and dad said nothing, as I took unending bites of what I was convinced would swell me.

When I was full – for real – my mom pointed at the small handful of fries I had left, and I ate them too, in pairs, trying not to let my damp cheeks dampen more than they already had.

With nothing left on the tray, I said "I'm full," in a broken whisper.

"Good," my mom said, relieved. "No more missing lunch, got it?"

I said, "Got it," but what I meant by that was, "I'm a void, now, fuck you."

They drove me home, then returned to their jobs and have-tos. But before starting in on my homework, I went to the back yard, wandered to where the fence was, and threw up less-than-I-hoped of the number two combo. And as I heaved – slobbery and out of breath – I felt the power in me shift out of its recesses in my gut and into the world in front of me, right where I could see it. Steamy, rancid power.

I wiped my face with the sleeve of my hoodie while I kicked snow over the vomit, then slowly wandered back into the house. I tossed the hoodie in the wash, then I brushed my teeth in my parents' bathroom out of spite. Some water splashed up onto the mirror, but I forgot about it and brushed my teeth again because I could still taste the vomit. After a third brushing, I returned my toothbrush to the holder in the bathroom down the hall, went down the stairs to through the dining room, and settled in the kitchen. My mom and dad came home a few hours later to me sitting at the breakfast bar, finishing the last of my math homework, and one less peppermint in the pantry.

On that strange Tuesday in February, my ritual of maintaining control began. I would eat, throw up, then suck on a piece of candy as both reward and taste-changer. This, of course, was even easier to get away with at school. I got my lunch, ate it, then threw it up in the boy's bathroom near the main entrance where Mrs. Rhytner couldn't follow me. Since there was no guarantee that all of it would come up, I filled the space between meals with excuses and over-complicated explanations to convince myself that any weight I gained was purely collateral damage. I knew it was working when Mrs. Rhytner stopped me in the hall and said, "It seems like things are going better!"

I smiled and said, "Thanks, you were a big help," and walked away with a lollipop stick hanging out of my mouth like a trophy.

By the end of sophomore year, when I became a sixteen-year-old with a little yellow truck, my parents didn't even question why I didn't have any birthday cake. They were convinced that this Ian, the one who ate all his meals and didn't want to die, was the only version of their son that existed. I was whoever I needed to be in front of those who demanded convincing, and no matter how close I got to breaking, I knew that no one could control what I ate, what I thought, or how I felt about things. It was easy.

I was candy-sweet like it was nothing.

7

When my dad cheated on my mom the first time, it wasn't with the mail clerk, Stacy, like everyone thought it would be. No, it was with Rebecca, the woman who worked in the insurance business office a few floors down from his own. This wasn't Rebecca's fault. She had no idea that my dad was married. And I only knew about Rebecca because of the fight my parents had over my dad's second affair with one of his clients. During the fight, my mom yelled "Did she know about us, or about your son!? Or did you keep her in the dark just like you did with Rebecca!?"

In that same month, I got my first cellphone. I was thirteen at the time and not the best at texting. I think it was because I hated texting, really, and thought it was impersonal, boring, and stilted. Kelly knew this about me, and told me several times how irritating it was (for her) to have a best friend so lacking in something second-natured. She moaned about it enough over the years to make anyone want to delete her number, but I was too guilt-prone to do anything like that. That's why I offered the idea that she and I become pen pals over the summer, and we could swap dumb stories while I was in California.

The first letter Kelly sent me arrived the day after Andrew's party. Alli and I were both off, but she joined some friends from the restaurant to shop around for a few hours. I was invited to go with her, but I wanted to stay back and lounge a bit. Also, Andrew hadn't texted yet, so I wanted to be alone in case he did. Alli didn't question any of it, though, but left me her car keys in case I wanted to "explore" the neighborhood. I had nothing better to do than pace around Alli's house and read the letter Kelly sent me.

The envelope was a bright pink and coated in stickers. I tore into it and even ripped a few of the stickers in the process. I quickly plucked the note out and let it fall open. She started the letter with a "Heeeey," and filled half a page with everything someone could expect from a first-time pen-paller: nothing much. But it was only the first letter, so I wasn't too critical of how most of it was composed of the rudimentary "not a lot is happening, hope you had a safe flight, can't wait to hear about how it's going," and whatever else falls in that category.

She did, however, send a printed-out photo of her and I at the pool several summers ago. It was the same summer that we thought we were going to make it as songwriters because she got some music software for her birthday, and I could write lyrics. And since we both knew that we couldn't sing, we made her younger sister sing whatever hit we wrote that hour.

I cringed at the photo, even if the times were good. I was shirtless, and I hated it, so I slid it back into the envelope. It got caught on a firm piece of cardstock, though, and I realized there was still more to Kelly's first letter – a $20 gift card. It wasn't to anywhere specific, so I set it next to my phone on the bed, put the pool photo back in the envelope with the letter, and set it on the dresser.

Excited to tell Kelly about my first authentic party experience (and little else), I pulled a clean sheet of stationery from my backpack and tried to write out my reply. I thanked her for the photo and mentioned how happy we looked in it. But I quickly scrapped it for another attempt that only mentioned how fun it was when we were so young to think that making music was actually going to be the start of something. I wrote about the party and how fun it was to be surrounded by so many people who didn't have a clue who I was, and how inspiring it was to look out at San Diego from the balcony. Alli was mentioned a bit. Kayla too. I only got as far as the botched tarot reading when my phone buzzed.

I grabbed the phone from the bed and saw Andrew's name light up on the small screen.

(Andrew)	Hey! What's up?
(Me)	not a lot lol you?
(Andrew)	Not a lot either haha
	Last night was fun.
	Thanks for that

<pre>
        (Me)   no problem
                          thanks to you too
                          i loved it
        (Andrew)   I'm glad!
</pre>

Embarrassed as hell and not knowing what else to say, I just sent a ":)" and closed my phone. Twenty minutes later, it buzzed again.

<pre>
        (Andrew)   Do you want to hang out?
</pre>

I read "Do you want to hang out?" over and over again before I finally replied with a short "when?"

<pre>
        (Andrew)   In an hour or so?
                          We could go see a movie
                          or something
        (Me)   yah sounds fun
</pre>

We made plans to meet up at a movie theater downtown, the one with the eagle statues stuck to the marquee, which made it look more like a church than a movie theater, so I abandoned the half-written letter to Kelly and started getting ready.

After a shower, I chose one of the new shirts Alli bought me and threw it on first. I grabbed the gift card from Kelly and Alli's keys off the counter, locked the door behind me, and ran to the car. I tossed the gift card onto the seat next to me and sped off toward the downtown world of San Diego.

Andrew was already waiting for me by the time I parked and found my way inside. I realized too late that I forgot my gift card on the seat of the car, so using it to splurge on candy was no longer an option. He waved me over, and we embraced in a short but balmy hug. We were close enough that when I pressed my cheek into his shoulder and breathed in, I could easily make out the scent of his sandalwood pine. I hoped he didn't think it was weird to have my cheek so close to his, but he pressed his own cheek into the crown of my head, which had me sighing. We even held hands when we walked through the emerald doors, and I didn't even care who saw us do it.

I won't say I *hated* superhero movies, but I certainly didn't enjoy them as much as Andrew did. It was like watching a gambler whoop and holler at some high-end horse race, and I was the unamused patron there for the sole purpose of being seen out and about with the variety of society. But even if I thought the movie was pointless, I loved watching Andrew's reactions. He was happy as ever, and I loved to see it. I loved it so much, actually, that I even questioned my own judgments, and made a mental note to not only look up what movie came before this one (we were watching a sequel, I didn't know), but to watch it so that I had even more to talk about with Andrew.

After the movie, Andrew walked me to the car. He saw it before I did, but when I also noticed that the passenger side window had been smashed in, I let out a "What the fuck!?" to match his "Oh shit."

I ran over to the car, jumping over a pothole in the parking lot, and looked around to see what was damaged or stolen. Most of it was completely untouched – aside from the window and its scattered shards – but the gift card Kelly gave me was gone.

"Who the hell breaks into a car for twenty bucks!?"

Andrew set his hand on my back. "It's California, dude, it happens."

"Alli's going to be so pissed," I said. And she was. I watched as my cousin inspected everywhere on the violated vehicle. The small group of work friends who drove her to the scene were all sitting motionless in their car while Andrew and I were just there and waiting for Alli to give any sort of direction.

"Alli, I'm so sorry. I–"

"It's fine, Ian," she snapped. "It happens."

I turned to Andrew and he shrugged.

"Oh thank God," Alli said, pulling out a handful of used scratch card lottery tickets from the middle console. Alli used to host a poker club when she was in college, but it got a little out of hand. Now, Alli gets her fix by buying lottery tickets and using them to offset the price of gas. "This sucks," she said.

I didn't see what the big deal was since only the window was busted, but that car was Alli's first "adult" purchase, and she loved it because of all the hard work it represented.

After about an hour of phone calls, Alli was given the number of a car rental place and the reference number to provide when she went to pick her car back up from the repair shop. Insurance covered all of it. We drove home in silence.

In her blatant stoicism, Alli said, "Don't *ever* leave shit in your car, Ian. Got it?" and went to bed, leaving me alone in the living room. I know it's not very admirable, but I was honestly more upset over my stolen gift card than I was about Alli's "Crimson Baby."

* * *

"You not really like this, I think."

"Like what?" I asked, burying my hand in a bag of chips. I felt around for a salty one while Yaryna slid the small dish of salsa toward me. We usually talked between the rushes and I was always impressed by her off-center considerations.

"Not real," she said.

"Not real?"

"Yes, like fake, maybe?"

"Fake? Yaryna I..." The words trailed off while I felt around for another chip. The teal blue salsa dish looked like a tide pool of red algae against the dark wood of the bar.

"What I'm saying is, I see how you want to be, and it is different from how you are. Like you don't always let yourself be that."

"Don't let myself be what? What are yo-"

"You are a *real* fake."

Yaryna's cold comment made me look up from the salsa dish. There was a language barrier between Yaryna and I, but I knew she wasn't being cruel. I filled the silence by munching on chips.

"I was a real fake too," she went on. "Never myself, always pretending. It's exhausting, though, right?"

"Maybe."

"Oh, I have something." Yaryna smoothed the wrinkles from her apron as she stood. "Hold on."

She left the breakroom while I stirred the salsa with a chip and waited. Yaryna wasn't gone long, but I had enough time to listen to most of what Pat and the line cook were arguing about by the time she came back.

"For you," she said, handing me an unwrapped book. It was a western, written in the 1940s by an author I didn't recognize but might have recognized if I paid better attention to a time outside from my own. Scanning the back, I could tell it wasn't a love story, at least, but the story of a man lost in the mountains and the journey he takes finding his way back.

"It is about real fake. You will see what I mean."

"Thanks, Yaryna."

"Yes, read when you have the time."

I nodded, then slid the novella into the front pocket of my apron.

* * *

Andrew continued to call me Lemon at work, and if I'm being honest, I loved it. Others caught on, and by the end of the week, I was Lemon to everybody – a name that I earned myself and didn't have to prove to anyone. Only the customers knew me as Ian, which made it even more special because the ones who called me Lemon knew me – like, *really* knew me – and I felt converted to a whole new self.

During the slow times, Alli, Andrew, and I would play *Hearts* with a deck of souvenir playing cards like so many reborn people do. The three of us talked about serious things like the people we used to be or what the hell was right and wrong with the world. I was surprised that there was always something new for us to talk about and how Andrew has such a careful way of pulling the authenticity out from under me. He made it so easy to talk about what made me who I was and how I let so many things get to me. No wonder Alli got along with him so well. Every part of him was genuine.

Andrew took me surfing on a breezy Saturday morning. I had no experience with surfing, but Andrew was sure he could at least get me to stand up on the board. We walked from his apartment to the beach, which I later found was why he lived there. As it turned out, Andrew taught surfing lessons on the weekends just to offset the cost of living in a state made of gold.

"I wasn't a good surfer when I started," he told me.

"Then how can you teach lessons?"

"You don't need to know how to surf to push people into waves." With a shove, I was coasting on the top of the small crest of ocean. I threw one of my feet forward, trying to land a smooth pop-up, like Andrew had me practice in the grass earlier that morning. My aim was wrong, or maybe it was the wrong foot, but I was thrown backwards into the wave. Under the water, I tossed once but was able to catch the sand with my foot and stand. I wiped the saltwater away from my eyes and nose. Gold flecks floated down with the sand. Andrew was laughing and waving a shaka. "Almost!" he called, in sarcasm-robustica.

I fell off my board several more times before finally standing for four whole seconds on the board, and I could feel in the core of my being why people took to surfing.

Coasting on waves with Andrew was worth the salt water up my nose and sore body, but after about an hour, I decided to sit on the beach and take in the Tourmaline Beach surf culture. The parking lot that led up from the shore was one of the only free all-day parking lots in the area, so it was packed. Jeff, who I met on the way from the car, was grilling hot dogs off the back of his pickup and directing traffic.

"This one's leavin'!" I heard him shout across the lot. He was waving over a Jeep and pointing to the silver car pulling out. Music boomed from portable speakers, which paired well with the smell of cooking meat and sunscreen.

Andrew was a marvel on the waves, and I was falling in love with the West Coast and the man I met in its reverie. Run after run, he coasted like no one else could. I was sure of it, because no one else out there looked as happy with themselves as he did. Maybe it was because he knew I was watching, but it didn't matter. I loved the way he got down real low on the board to dip his hand in the water; feeling the ripples move through his fingers. He threw his arms out, wingspan, and when he looked up at me, smiling through the brine, I knew that there was nowhere else I wanted to be.

* * *

"Well, you gotta believe in *somethin'!*"

Sarah's hair was in two braids that hung over her shoulders, and I liked the purple ribbon she tied into the one on her left side. She was the God-fearing new hire from Tennessee who didn't last a week before Alli convinced her of a nose piercing. It was four in the afternoon, and Alli and I were trying to teach her the rules of *Hearts*, but that quickly turned into a long-winded discussion about the universe and who exactly watched over it.

"I never said I didn't," I said. "I just don't need to figure it out."

"Oh, so you're one of *those* people."

"*Those* people?"

"Yah. People who think, 'oh, it's just life and it'll be over before we know it, so let's not waste time trying to, I don't know, learn how it all works.'"

"So what?" I said and took a prideful sip of iced tea.

"Don't you wonder where we all came from?"

"Not really."

"So that's the real waste!"

"How?"

"Well," she said, tossing a braid back behind her shoulder. "You're given a life – whether you want it or not – and you spend it not even caring how it all happened? I don't think so."

"I know how it happened. My mom lied about the birth control, and–"

"Ew, stop. You know what I mean."

"Okay," I said. "So, you think that since we're here already, and it's not up to us how we got here, it's our responsibility to find out why?"

"Exactly!"

"No."

Sarah pursed her lips and shrugged. "Well, my table's food is probably ready, soooooo I'm gonna go get it."

"Go for it. But don't ask the burger where it came from! It's *brutal!*"

I got better at serving, and I'm not just saying that because I was more comfortable with who I was becoming. I saw the proof of it in lofty tips and in little notes left at the bottom of receipts. People had a good time, and I was so thrilled. Andrew taught me how to say things like "I threw a few extra fries on there for you" so that the customers would feel special. And during the slower times, between lunch and dinner when people were running around the city looking for anything but food, Andrew and I would sneak around and prove how good we were at breathing together; it's what we did best. My favorite place to meet him was in the neon alley where the lights made it so much more magical than the backside of the parking lot or the cramped space on the other side of the building. Those neon lights were all we needed to see how powerful we were together.

Some days, I would go home with more than a couple hundred bucks in tips alone, and I loved folding up bills and fitting them in my apron. It felt ritualistic, at the end of my shift, to take the bills out of my apron, make them all face the same way, and cash out. And that was how Andrew's poetry began finding its way to me.

After a half shift, I cashed out and went to throw my apron up in the server's station. Lodged into the wooden seams of my assigned piece of shelf was a folded piece of paper with pieces of dried flowers pressed into the fibers. And on the front of it, "Lemon" was written out in a beautiful, fine tip cursive. I was so careful not to tear it when I opened it, and I'm glad I was, because I wasn't always a careful person, and this was deserving of all formal attention.

On the note was a one-line poem left for me in purple ink from one of Andrew's pens, and it was beautiful. Using the dome light above me, I held up the paper and let the light shine on its backside. Sunflowers and daisies stood pronounced against the light. I brought the poem down to my face to see if I could smell the flowers, but it smelled instead like old books. The scent was a complete contrast to the flowers in such a beautiful, floral masculinity that rendered accretions of raw humanity.

Read me like you listen to music

Though it was only a single line, there wasn't a syllable that didn't mean absolutely everything to me. I folded the poem just like he did, longways then short, making sure his words wouldn't crease in my pocket. I grabbed a pen and a piece of paper from the notebook in my apron and used the wall to write a poem back to him. After writing something about an orchid blossom on the edge of a glass, I signed "Love, Lemon" at the bottom and slipped it into the front pocket of his apron.

By returning a poem to Andrew, a ritualistic pattern of writing poems for each other began. We were experts at timing it right so that there was always a new poem to read at the start of the shift, even on the days we didn't work together. And on the days that we shared a shift, we traded poetry in passing and paired them with winks, smiles, and even short, quick kisses.

Poetry buried my everything, including the half-written letter I was supposed to send Kelly days ago. There were pages of Andrew's poetry on the dresser, in my pockets, and on the windowsill (where I kept my favorite ones). And at night, when my thoughts of him clashed against thoughts of what would happen if my parents found about him, I knew that I could unfold a piece of paper, read it in the light from my phone, and let his poetry bury my mind as well.

8

Cavities: hollow and sore with no other fix than fillings or crowns, and I had three of them by the time I was seventeen. Another two came a month or so before graduation. Five used-to-be good teeth (four molars and one canine) filled or crowned in chrome. I wasn't surprised at all by the number of cavities, though. Candy and vomit are far from fluoride.

"This isn't cheap," my mom said the day I got my fifth tooth fixed. The left side of my face was still numb. "But it's not healthy, either. You need to take better care of your teeth."

I thought about telling her how many times a day I brushed my teeth (paranoid of bad breath that I *never* let happen) or how I carried an extra toothbrush with me to school. Instead, I just nodded while she spoke about some cousin I never met.

"She lost two teeth on the left side, but they were close enough to the front where you could see it, the hole in her smile, and she was so embarrassed by it that she never even smiled for pictures. Sammy didn't like to talk much, or laugh, which I think was sad, but when she did, she would cover her mouth with her hand so no one could see it. So please, Ian, take care of yourself."

Her story stood out to me because my mom talked about her family more than the cost of things, and that was rare. The other reason was because I was able to see a side of my mom that I didn't see a lot of the time anymore – the side of her that was trying, in some way, to reach me through the void. As rare as it was, I appreciated the way it reminded me of our lives before it changed. Before I was different people all at once. Before we didn't have to try so hard to understand each other.

I felt the fixed teeth with my tongue as I walked around San Diego like I did on most of my days off. Alli got her car back but decided to keep the rental for the rest of the summer so that I would have something to get around in. I still preferred to walk around, though, and observe the buildings, billboards, other people's conversations, and the overall business of the city.

Billboards always intrigued me because they were so high up, for one, and I liked the way faded pictures looked. Things are more interesting when you have to look up to see them, and I think that's why we like the stars so much, or why we look up at the snow when it falls instead of staring ahead or down at it on the ground. To me, walking around San Diego while looking up at billboards was like watching the northern lights, which

I was sure were less impressive than billboards because billboards had more colors, and I didn't have to freeze.

One day, I was lucky enough to watch a crew of three men peel away the massive sheets of vinyl to reveal the steel behind it. I watched as they replaced the sign with an advertisement for fresh oysters, lobster, shrimp, and other sea-dwellers available as appetizers at some seafood place. I had never had oysters before on account of Colorado's insistent inaccessibility to anything other than beef and chicken, so I decided to make "eating an oyster for the first time" my afternoon pursuit.

After a bit of ambling, I discovered that the place advertised on the billboard was nowhere near downtown San Diego and was instead somewhere closer to L.A. So, I settled on a small seafood restaurant on the endcap of the block. It was called Martin's, which I, after looking at it, thought was completely undetectable if I weren't intentionally trying to find a place like it. But the prices were reasonable, and that means a lot for a place like Martin's.

Simple and navy were the only two things that defined the physicality of Martin's. There was nothing outstanding about the restaurant's interior, and it seemed bare compared to the other places I'd been to. What was there, though, was painted or accented in a deep navy blue like the whole of it had been curated from the Pacific's own deep lithography. I appreciated its nauticality and was drawn specifically to the fishing nets that clung to the bar at the far end of the room.

There were maybe seventeen individual tables, and none of them sat more than four aside from the six-top in the center of the small dining room. On each table were salt and pepper shakers with dried sea sponges between them. A lone waitress hurried in and out of the kitchen bringing deep fried appetizers and drinks to loud people.

I noticed right away that there were no open seats at Martin's, and not even The Gilded Naupaka ever felt as busy as Martin's did. I know we got busy sometimes, but if we weren't seating anyone, it was because the cooks needed to catch their breath and not because the tables were full. Martin's was packed.

After waiting a reasonable while for a table, I was finally seated in a booth by the window. The menus were stuck under thick glass embedded in the wood, and I tried not to think too hard about the grimy smudges on the paper. Paige, the waitress, had a messy bun that sat lopsided on her head. She was covered in freckles and looked like she caught whatever was on the menu that morning with her bare hands.

"Never been here before, have ya?" she asked, though it sounded more like a statement than a question. I shook my head.

"How did you know?"

"I own it," she replied, pouring the iced tea I ordered into a hard plastic cup with ice. "So I'm here every day, and it's your first time in."

I nodded. "First time, ya."

Paige smiled, self-amused and for good reason. I was impressed that someone could remember enough faces to know that I wasn't one of them. She said, "I'll be right out with the oysters," and left through a pair of navy-dyed satin panels.

When Paige came back with a silver tray, I was surprised at how much shell there was compared to meat. Both pieces of the sea seemed to swallow the briny mixture, and though the exteriors were uneven, the bumps and grooves of the shell kept themselves balanced flat. I prodded the oyster meat with my fork and thought to myself, *is this really where pearls come from?*

I doused them both in lemon juice then tilted one of them into my mouth. In regards to flavor, the oyster meat was salty, and I liked that a lot. If there was a texture to it, I didn't know because I swallowed it all in one smooth pass while I listened in on the group of three women behind me. It sounded like they all used to group up in the area, or at least attended the same school. One mentioned how long it had been since all of them were together, so I turned around briefly to get a glance at whose stories I was listening to.

All three women looked to be in their thirties, maybe forties, and they were all smiling over their drinks as if they had been poured by gods. One of the women covered her mouth when she smiled, though, and I noticed that it was because she was missing one of her incisors. This is something people do when they don't like their smile. They cover it. And since there is no way to keep ourselves from smiling when the impulse is too great or friendships are too strong, the only option is to smile behind cupped hands.

While letting the voices of the three women get lost in the broad sea of restaurant noise, I placed the two oysters' shells face down on the tray – it seemed like the right thing to do – and thought about how similar pearls are to teeth.

* * *

The first Greek hero was Cadmus. He was the maker of men, bringer of the alphabet, and was slaying monsters long before Zeus' golden boy Heracles ever did. Cadmus set the bar for what a hero should be.

After plucking the teeth from the jaw of a dragon, Cadmus buried them, and from the teeth grew an army of strong men who knew their worth and fought against each other to prove it. The dragon had been guarding a spring of fresh water before Cadmus took its life, and I only mention that because it was the Fourth of July, and the day was so hot that I also would have killed a dragon for water.

Most of us were scheduled to work a double shift so that we at The Gilded Naupaka could keep up with the number of customers pouring in from inland states to spend their money in the west. Our sections were cut in half, which was fine because it was the busiest that we had ever been, and by noon I made as much as I would have during a regular double shift. Alli came up with a special drink, and Yaryna even learned how to fold paper boats for the kids. The heat was really something, and I was so glad to have an indoor section. Andrew was serving on the patio, but Alli told me he asked for it because he didn't want to be stuck inside when the fireworks went off.

Though we were all exhausted and counting down the hours before closing, it was a fun, busy day filled with music and other people's money. And when the sun finally set, and the fireworks began their display, I leaned against the bar to watch the artificial supernovas burst and fizzle through the charred air.

"What's up with Andrew?" Alli asked.

"What do you mean?"

"Look at him." Alli nodded toward a clearly distraught Andrew storming toward us with an untouched bottle of beer.

"It's too warm, I guess," he said, setting the dewy bottle down on the bar with a heavy breath. "This guy is pissing me off."

I looked over at the table and saw the family of five; a man, his wife, and three kids. Each family member was fully covered in red, white and blue, proving their manic patriotism. Two of the children were in a hitting match with each other while the third slid silverware off the table and onto the patio floor. Their mom, who was sitting right next to them, was too busy flipping through photos on her camera to care about what her children were doing. And at the head of the table sat a large, proud man who looked as if he was drawn to life from some all-American caricature. His meaty arms swelled out from under the short sleeves of his t-shirt, and his barrel-like torso warped the stars and stripes that decorated it. I watched him shovel food into his bright red face while listening to Andrew and Alli talk. Their conversation drifted in and out of the fireworks, so I only heard the last of it.

"But isn't Pat from the Philippines?" Alli asked.

"That's what I told him!" Andrews' words were quick and sharp. "But he said 'I don't care what part of China he's from' and wouldn't even *look* at Pat when he asked for his drink order."

Alli said, "I'll have Carol check on Pat. Good luck, dude." She handed Andrew a new beer and a chilled glass from the fridge. Andrew shrugged then made his way back to the table while Alli went to find Carol. I stayed at the bar, though, and watched in repulse as the man at the head of the table grabbed Andrew's arm and scolded him. Andrew wrested his arm away, which made the man throw his napkin on the table and stand. Compared to Andrew, he was shorter but much more muscular. Andrew didn't move, but I saw his mouth moving rapidly. He was trying to fight fire with reason, I thought, but the man was not listening.

The man got in Andrew's face, jabbed his finger into his chest, and yelled, "Shut up, faggot!"

Andrew swung his fist, landing it directly on the man's square jaw. In the light of the fireworks, I watched a pearly tooth pop out of the man's mouth, bounce two or three times, then land next to one of the many spoons under the table.

The man did not swing back. Instead, he put three fingers to the corner of his lip and glared at Andrew with a look of horror. No one had ever swung at him before. He didn't even know what to do.

The whole patio fell silent. Carol, who came out to the patio right as Andrew punched the man, stared wide-eyed at the sea of people who also just watched a server punch a customer. I could tell she was struggling to make a move. We all stood frozen as Carol lock eyes with Andrew, dying to know what she would do about it. She said, "Go home. You're done." Guilt flooded her face, and we all could tell she didn't feel right about it either.

Andrew tried to say something, but Carol put her hand up, stopping him. As Carol turned from Andrew to console the man and his family, Andrew threw his apron down and left through the back patio gate. Alli grabbed up his apron, and I followed her behind the bar. She took a rubber band from around one of the pen holders, wrapped up Andrew's tips, and put it in the front pocket of my apron.

"Make sure he gets this, okay?"

In minutes, the patio continued its usual thrum, and the family of five returned to eating their (compensated) meal. The man was chewing a lot slower, and I couldn't help laughing.

"What's so funny?" Alli asked.

"Nothing," I said, but I knew that even though he got Andrew fired, that man would have to start hiding his smile.

9

"Let's go swimming," was all Andrew said when I called to tell him I had his tips. By the time I clocked out, the clock on my phone read 12:07 A.M. and I was the second to last server to leave. Even though Alli asked if I wanted her to stay and close with me, I knew it was a long day for everyone and figured she would want to head home. Besides, I had the rental car.

Andrew never left the parking lot. He was sitting on the roof of his car and staring out at the city, so I climbed up next to him. Occasionally, a straggling firework went off, but I wasn't feeling patriotic in the least. I handed him the cash wad.

"Thanks. Ready to swim?"

"What?" I laughed, assuming it was a joke. "Yeah, let me just grab my suit."

"I'll drive."

"Oh, you're serious!" I blurted, as he got into the driver seat of his navy-blue car.

"Sure am! Ever been to the Coves?" He got into the car without an answer from me and shut the door.

Confused but curious, I went around to the passenger side and slid in. All over his dashboard was the poetry I wrote him – piles of little paper burying it just like his poetry buried my dresser and windowsill. I wondered how many there were or whether he kept them in any special order as we drove off toward the Coves.

The Coves was a small but luxurious resort situated near the coast. It wasn't far from The Gilded Naupaka, and I only really knew about it because some of our customers liked to brag about their accommodations. Andrew parked in front of a large, white fence that spanned across a small section of the parking lot. I noticed that the main entrance was closed, but if tracing around cities with Andrew had taught me anything, it was that closed entrances meant nothing to someone as forthright and free as him.

"Where are you going?" I asked, as he headed toward the fence. Andrew turned back at me and smiled as if he knew I was going to ask him that. He shook his head, humored by my naivety, and hoisted himself up and over the wooden planks. I heard him slide down the other side before landing in the soft grass.

"Hurry up!" he whisper-yelled through the slits in the fence. Of course, I wasn't going to be left out of whatever it was Andrew had in mind, so I jumped up, grabbed the top of the fence, and pulled myself over.

I was fascinated by how bright the other side of the fence was. I could see well enough, but the only artificial light came from the parking lot and a small lamp outside of a door that led to the main resort lobby. The moon, however, was stuck on us and gave enough light for us to find our way around.

In the small courtyard, I was able to make out two shapes; each separated by grass and surrounded by concrete tile. They were pools, and I assumed the smaller of the two was a hot tub. Squinting, I watched Andrew as he folded back the cover of the hot tub, took off all of his clothes, and slid into the warm water.

We weren't just going swimming like any casual escapade, I realized, but instead sneaking into a resort, at midnight, and skinny-dipping in its courtyard pools. *So what?* I thought and began pulling my own clothing off. I was careful not to let my metal belt buckle clang against the tile, then joined Andrew in the small pool.

"It's nice," I said, not yet comfortable with the quiet.

Andrew nodded and leaned his head back on the edge of the tub. At this new angle, I was able to see his shoulders, his arms, the small bends in his chest, and the whole of his upper physicality. As he breathed, droplets of water would run over the tattoo that sat just above his right clavicle: *Do Not Embalm.*

"You don't want to be buried?" I asked.

"What do you mean?"

"Your tattoo."

"Which one?"

I pointed to his chest, wondering what others he had and if I would be lucky enough to see them.

"Oh," he said. "That doesn't mean I don't want to be buried. It means I better be the same *me* when it happens. No chemicals or wires. Just me, as I am, right into the ground."

"Can you even do that? I thought you had to be embalmed, like, legally."

"Depends. Some places will let you be buried in just a cloth, or in a wooden box, so you can join the earth again."

"Wouldn't you do that anyway?" I asked, still confused about why it was such a big deal.

"No, not really. They put too much steel and concrete between your body and the soil, so there's no way you could ruin the landscaping." He paused for a moment, looking upwards. "I'd like to be a tree, maybe." I think he was emotional about it, because he cleared his throat like people do when they don't want to cry, and then said plainly, "It's a full moon."

I followed his eyes to the not-yet-full moon. "It's a waxing gibbous."

"Wooooow, we've got a moon expert on our hands!" Though sarcastic, he wasn't cruel.

"I'm obsessed! When I was in eighth grade, I went outside every night for a whole month just to write down the moon phases. I used a special calendar my mom got me, but I also kept track in a little notebook because I'm thorough like that. I can tell right away what kind of moon it is, even when it looks full."

Andrew laughed. "That's adorable."

"It's true! Sometimes I– " Andrew stopped my lips with his, and I let him; I welcomed it, even, because we were naked in a hot tub beneath the glow of a not-yet-full moon. Under the water, I felt Andrew's hand reach around my waist while he set the other on my left thigh and squeezed lightly. I closed my eyes as he kissed my cheek and behind my ear before making his way down the curve of my neck and across my chest. He rolled my nipple in his teeth while I slid my hands up his back and pressed kisses into his left shoulder and neck. At once, I wasn't so afraid of my free body. I was alive in it. The most alive I could ever be, because the body I knew from the mirror was gone, and the body that Andrew touched was new to us both.

I moved around to sit above him, and he leaned forward to kiss my waist. The air above the water was cold on my bare torso and arms, and I shivered. Andrew noticed and started to splash the warm water onto me, which made us both laugh. We must have been too loud because a light from a window lit up the courtyard.

"Hey!" a voice called from the window. Andrew and I turned to look and saw a resort employee silhouetted in the light. We both jumped out of the water, neither of us willing to answer, and I couldn't have cared less because I was having fun and didn't owe it to anyone else. Andrew grabbed his keys off the ground and ran toward the fence while I tried gathering our clothes.

"Leave 'em!" Andrew hollered, so I took my debit card and ID out of my pocket and chased after him, laughing as I billowed the California night in and out of my lungs. I made it over the fence just as the door to the courtyard opened. The resort employee was still hollering at us from the other side of the fence when Andrew tossed his keys to me and jumped into the passenger side. I got in the driver's seat and sped out of the parking lot, knowing we made it. We could have been anyone.

"Let's go to my place," he said, out of breath. "Do you know how to get there from here?"

"No idea." I replied. The grin on my face felt as wide as the coast.

"Okay, go left up here and take the highway a few miles. Then turn onto the freeway and it will take us home."

I nodded and Andrew leaned his head against the seat. I watched the streetlights glow over him as we drove. In my mind, I repeated the same three words over and over.

Highway. Freeway. Home.

* * *

I woke up in Andrew's bed wearing some gym shorts that he let me borrow, and I was happy wondering how many more mornings like it I would get to have before the end of the summer. Andrew wasn't in the bed, but I could hear him in the kitchen making noises with the dishes. The clanging of the silverware drawer reminded me of railway cars.

Rolling over, I repositioned myself on my forearm and reached across to my phone on the nightstand. The battery died the night before, but I didn't have a charger for it. I set the unresponsive phone back down on top of my ID and debit card, got out of bed, and looked around Andrew's room. I hadn't been there since his birthday party, so in the morning glow I could see more of the things he kept around.

The walls were all a sandy pink, aside from an accent wall painted in rich emerald. There were some posters hung around, and a large red and gold tapestry with a crease through the left side peaked out from behind the headboard. On the nightstand was an old-fashioned alarm clock, some change, three or four lollipops, and a to-do list written on a dollar bill.

To the right of the closet door was a floor length mirror, and next to it was a longboard. It was scuffed up and worn, and I couldn't tell what the design on it was because he had covered most of it in stickers. But aside from the posters, the longboard, and tapestry, there wasn't much to Andrew's room. It was all so open and clear with bold marks of individuality.

"Sleep well?" Andrew asked, as I ambled into the kitchen. He was sitting on the breakfast bar with his bare feet resting on the back of one of the barstools and a sandwich in his hand.

"Yeah, actually." I yawned. "Thanks for the shorts."

"No problem," he said. "Keep 'em."

"What are you eating?"

"Grilled cheese," he said. "Want one?"

I looked over at the clean stove, and it was clear that it hadn't been used. No frying pan sat on the back burner or in the sink. Andrew pointed at the microwave. "I'm good," I said, amused. "Hey, I wanna talk about last night." He sat up, concerned.

"Was it bad?" he asked.

"No, not at all!" I blurted. "Actually, I think...I want to do more...with you."

Andrew looked confused. I was so bad at talking about sex. "You want to go swimming again?" he asked.

"Sorta," I said. "But I want more of the other stuff too."

"Huh, okay... Like what?"

I stared up at the ceiling, going through everything I wanted to do with Andrew, then settled on one that I thought would be more manageable. I went to his room and grabbed two lollipops from the pile.

"Well, we've done this," I said, placing the lollipops down on the counter mirroring each other. "But would you want to try this?" I inverted one of the lollipops so that instead of facing each other in a kissing scenario, they were facing each other's stick.

"Looks fun," he slowed, setting out his hand. I put my hand in his open palm and he lifted it to his lips. Amused, I was thankful that I wasn't scheduled to work that day.

I rested my head against his shoulder and could feel his heartbeat through my cheek. We stayed like that for a while – just holding each other and breathing in the warmth of the morning.

Later, Andrew drove me to Alli's so I could get a new change of clothes and my phone charger, then drove me all the way back down to Ocean Beach to get the rental car back. Alli must have seen us from the patio bar as we drove up, because by the time Andrew parked Alli was standing cross-armed and fuming at the side of the rental.

"Where the fuck have you been!?" she blurted. The edges of her ears were red. This happened a lot when Alli was a kid, but later it only happened when she was really, really pissed off.

"I was with Andrew," I said, "and my phone died."

She looked at Andrew then back at me. "He has my number, too," she said. I tried to say something, but she cut me off. Even if I was trying to apologize, she wouldn't let me. "Look, Ian, I don't need to know where you are all of the time, but you're staying with me at my house, and I would have liked to not have stayed up worrying about you."

I said, "Fine, sorry," and left.

Back at Alli's, I took a long shower while I let my phone charge. When it was charged enough to turn back on, I saw that I had two texts and four missed calls. All four of the missed calls and one of the texts were from Alli. The other text was from Kelly.

> (Kelly)   hey Ian.
>
>   idk if you got the card i sent

a few weeks ago
but i haven't gotten
 anything from you yet. did
you send one? it probably
got lost if you did
but if you didn't can i ask
 why? i never hear
from you anymore, but if
you don't want to
talk to me anymore i get it
but can you at least
let me know?? :(

If I wasn't so frustrated with Alli, I might have done things differently. But at the time, I thought everyone was asking too much of me, which made me text reckless things like "Don't be so damn dramatic, I got busy" to my best friend.

Years would pass before I heard from her again, but that's on me.

* * *

I was getting pretty sick of my music. Skip, skip, repeat. Maybe shuffle? No. Nothing was worth listening to, and I needed something new. I yanked out my headphones, wrapped them around my mp3 player, and tossed it on the floor. It landed short of the "clean" clothes pile, but I didn't bother worrying about things like that.

Alli was on my nerves. I avoided her the whole rest of the evening until I didn't want to hang out alone in

96

my room anymore listening to the same damn songs for no damn reason. I put on my hoodie and a new pair of socks, then wandered into the living room where I knew Alli would be. She was hunched over folders and sticky notes like the hell of a planner she was.

Alli, as it turns out, was pretty frustrated with me too. She said it right away, and I didn't even have to ask.

"Not gonna lie, Ian," she said. "I want to talk about what happened."

"It's not my fault," I said. "I didn't smash the window, some—"

"That's the problem, Ian. You think that just because it wasn't your fault you don't have anything to do with it."

"Yeah, I don't."

"But it's the way you *act* about it! Like you don't even care."

"Hey, my money got stolen! I'm—"

"It was *twenty fucking bucks*, Ian, come on." Her ears were red. Though her voice was controlled, her ears were burning. "And now this thing with Andrew?"

I fell quiet and my gut sank. I hadn't told Alli about Andrew, but she knew somehow. And she said it, out loud. Would she hate me for it? Would it get all the way back to my parents now?

"Look at me," she said, slowly.

I lifted my eyes from the grooves in the table and met her at her gaze.

"Why won't you talk about it with me?"

"I don't know."

"You can talk to me, Ian, I love you." Salt water built up under my eyes, and I accepted the grip that California life had on me. But there was an honesty to her that still somehow gave me room to breathe. Alli poured two glasses of wine.

"My parents don't know."

"Oh," she said. "Would they...understand?" Alli paused a bit before *understand* like she already knew they weren't capable of it. Understanding, acceptance, unconditional love...all of these things that parents promise to give but can't, sometimes, because not even their own parents knew what it meant.

"They broke my computer."

"What do you mean?"

"My computer. For school. My dad broke it in half."

Maybe I was feeling recklessly honest, hunched over the glass of wine. Or maybe Alli was the right type of person to tell things to because she didn't make you feel like shit for feeling the way you feel. Yeah. That was it.

"There was this guy I was talking to a while back. Last winter. He lived in New York, but we met at a student conference in Chicago. Young Leaders in Business, or something like that. We would message each other in a separate group chat, and I used my school computer for video calls. But my parents didn't know. I didn't think they would have a problem with it, really, but..." I stopped, collected my breaths, and pushed through the sludge of words. "...but they did have a problem with it – with me. My dad...he found me on a video call with Tyler. It was really late, I guess I was talking loud or something. We weren't doing anything, just chatting, but my dad could tell what was going on, and before I knew it my laptop was snapped in half. My mom came in and asked what was happening, and it just spiraled. They told me that I was a 'Marlow' and Marlows are good people who don't choose to live 'that way.' So now I have to work to pay off the school's laptop, and they made me claim it was an accident."

"Oh wow," Alli said.

Oh wow, for sure. We each took a silent sip of our wine. There was a long moment of quiet, but not an uncomfortable one because it was filled with contemplation. Room to breathe.

I thought about how miserable I was going to be in California. Then I thought about how wrong I was to think that. And after Alli said "Oh wow," I realized how thankful I was for the opportunity. The prospect of it all that I didn't see before. I was weightless in California.

"Thank you," I said.

"For what?"

"For everything. Letting me live here, for the job, and for..." I don't know why I let the words fall short. She knew – I knew she knew – but I was blushing and nervous about it all, still not having said it out loud.

"For Andrew?"

"Yes, for Andrew," I rolled my eyes but my smile showed her that I really didn't mind her saying it for me.

"He likes you," she told me.

"Oh yeah?" My cheeks were warm with it.

She looked right at me and whispered, "Yeah."

10

With Andrew gone, Carol needed someone to pick up the slack. But as Carol and the rest of the staff soon came to realize, Zach's application grossly oversold his capabilities. Zach zipped around the restaurant in a panicked speed-walk and had a bad habit of taking over tables that weren't in his section. He didn't mean to, I don't think, because he couldn't remember where the server sections were. So, as kind as Zach was, there was no way he would have been able to fill Andrew's shoes.

We helped where we could, and soon Zach was doing alright. I offered to work that Thursday, just in case Zach needed help with the large bachelorette party that was booked weeks ago. It was for sixteen people, but he said he could handle it. I was relieved because I was tired from the busy week. Besides, I had a gift to bake for Andrew.

I was in my gray shirt, the one with the small bleach stain on the front left side that kept me from wearing it outside the house. I kept the shirt for things like cleaning or working in the kitchen.

What started as a small interest in baking transformed into a love for it, and I loved to bake cupcakes, specifically, because full cakes were too much to worry about. Cupcakes had an endearing simplicity that I found aesthetically satisfying.

I brought cupcakes to school, in small cardboard boxes, and passed them out to friends or teachers who I thought needed one. I took cupcakes to work with me at the diner and left them out for the other servers and cooks to snack on. Cupcakes were, like me, too sugary to be taken seriously. I liked that.

Wiping my frosting-coated fingers off on my gray shirt, I smiled. Finally, the color of the frosting was the perfect burnt orange. I picked the most symmetrical cupcake from the baking sheet and swirled the frosting on top in a smooth, effortless motion. The orange complimented the pink cake perfectly. I put the unfrosted ones to the side because even though I baked a whole batch, I only needed one.

A cupcake is not the most exciting belated-birthday gift, but Andrew seemed like the kind of person who would appreciate it anyway. I was very intentional with the coloring and decoration. He told me that orange was his favorite color, so I made the frosting a kind-yet-bold burnt orange. I had yellow sprinkles to put on top, but I chose to leave them off. The orange was just fine on its own. It was my trademark move to mix whipped marshmallow in with the frosting to make it lighter than frosting should be. The pink color of the cake was achieved by mixing pink gelatin mix in with the vanilla batter. It turned out to be the perfect shade of pink to match the pink stucco coating the exterior of The Lunetta. I put the cupcake in a small box I made from the paper I was supposed to write Kelly's letters on. Oh well.

The Lunetta, a three-star hotel stuck at the far end of San Diego, hired Andrew a few days earlier. Managing the front desk of a three-star hotel was such a sidestep from serving at The Gilded Naupaka, but Andrew was one of those people who didn't let their occupation define them. He knew who he was and that was all there was to it.

I agreed to meet him in the lobby of The Lunetta at around one o'clock so that we would have enough time to make it to our two-thirty lunch reservation. The cupcake was a surprise, though. I cradled the small box in my palms, paying careful attention to how tightly I held it. It felt wrong to hold it in the intense direct sunlight, so I turned it away from the large west-facing window in the lobby. That way, the sun could only peak around the edges of my shoulders.

Even though most of the paint had chipped off the trim, and the tile floor was stained and splotchy from water damage, the hotel was still just as inviting, which was impressive. Everything in San Diego is impressive. Even the less glamorous things like rundown hotels and ordering on foot from the drive through window were impressive in their own way.

There were others in the lobby, too, and I loved being absorbed into the hotel lobby crowd because unlike the nicer hotels, these people were loud and filled the room with life. "I can't, I'm allergic to coconut," I heard someone say, while another person was on the phone listing all of the places they looked for their lost wallet. I sighed, thankful that I didn't have to worry about coconut allergies or lost wallets. I was concerned only with the cupcake I brought with me to surprise the king of California.

I heard Andrew yell "Lemon! This way." I held the cupcake box close to my chest; there was no way I was going to let it get crushed. We made it through the crowd, down the hall, and finally to my car.

"Ready to eat?" he asked, climbing into the passenger seat.

"As long as I don't have to climb up buildings with a cupcake," I joked, handing him the sunset confection.

"Oh, what's this?" he said, then paused after opening the box. He looked at the colors with a grin before taking a huge bite of frosting and cake.

"Remember when you asked what I wanted to do with my life?"

"Yeah."

"Well, I think I have an answer."

"Oh ya?" he said through a mouthful of cake.

"Travel."

Andrew looked at me with a smirk, and I could tell that my answer surprised him. I knew he was expecting me to say something more responsible, but I wasn't in any place to consider responsibility. He said "Sounds magical." Then, his eyes grew wide, and he shouted, "I LOVE THIS SONG!"

Andrew turned the volume knob all the way to the right and stood up in the rental's open sunroof. He threw his arms up and yelled the lyrics into the open wind like it was a gospel. I threw my right arm around his leg to support him and kept my left hand on the wheel, but I was so distracted I missed the exit.

"You're really like this, aren't you!?" I hollered up to him.

"Like what!?" he hollered back. His hair was flying in the currents of the freeway, and between the wind, the music, and my mind, I was surprised he even heard me.

"Free!"

* * *

"Do you think I want to be famous!?"

The sun was vehement as it poured over the parking lot, resurrecting heat waves from the scalding metal roofs of the cars. Most people pretended not to hear him, but the ones that did look over at the yelling man quickly looked away again, shaking their heads. He was old; I could tell by the way he stood hunching over with one shoulder jutting out further than the other. Days in the sun had weathered his skin and yellowed his beard, which made him look even older than he probably was.

"I don't!" the man went on, squinting in the heat of the harangue and stomping his foot against the tarry lot. "I don't want to be famous! I don't want to be famous!"

Anyone watching could tell that there was no way that old man in mismatched shoes was in danger of fame. But he was so truly *terrified* by the idea of it, that his only salvation was to yell in front of a grocery store instead of standing on some corner with the other avenue vagabonds and their cardboard signs.

I was in my car going over the list of things I had to get from the store, listening to the hollering man through the rolled down window. It was a decently sized list made up of mostly food items, but there were a few things I added to the list myself. The new keypad system was being installed at Alli's place, so I offered to get the groceries on my way home from work. It was a divide-and-conquer sort of a deal as well as an attempt to show Alli I could contribute.

I had exactly $217 cash– $100 from home and $117 from my morning shift. I folded up the list and shoved the bills, in no order whatsoever, into my pocket. I didn't carry a wallet, but neither did the yelling man, so I handed him a fistful of uncounted bills on my way into the store.

As the automatic doors swung apart, a gust of cool air rinsed away the heat. Maybe I just expected it to be busier than it was, since the parking lot was packed, but I had no problem maneuvering the linoleum lanes.

Thirty minutes of shopping later, I had half a pantry of food and a complete stock of cleaning supplies and toiletries slotted next to each other in the cart. I couldn't find the brand of floor cleaner Alli asked for, so I settled for its generic counterpart. I was just leaving the cleaning aisle when my phone rang. Even though I didn't recognize the number, I answered.

"Ian! Hey!"

I couldn't tell who it was by the voice. "I'm sorry, who is this?"

"Aunt Lou!"

Of course. No one spoke with such a cadence and rhythm as she did, and I was embarrassed that it had been so long since we last spoke that I wouldn't remember what she sounded like. I said, "Oh, hey Aunt Lou!" while I made my way to the office supplies aisle for notecards and pens.

"I asked Alli for your number, I hope that's okay."

"Ya, that's fine. What's up?"

"Oh, you know, just calling to say hello and see how you've been. Are you having fun? Alli says you're doing a good job at the Naupaka."

"Oh yeah?" I said. Alli was a kind person, but she didn't go out of her way to say nice things to people's faces. I appreciated the round-about compliment. "It's been interesting, but I'm having a good time."

She said "Glad to hear it!" in all the enthusiasm I remembered about her. "Your parents might like it too, then! They're thinking of coming out in a week or so!"

I froze, creasing the notecards in my hand. "Wait, out here? Like, to San Diego?"

"More like to L.A. but yes. You all can stay at my place!"

"Sounds fun," I faked, and sideways-tossed the shrink-wrapped deck of notecards into the cart.

"Should be," Aunt Lou said. "It will be nice seeing everyone."

"Yeah," I said, trailing off.

"Well, I'll let you go, but I've been talking it over with Alli. I'll keep ya posted. Love you!"

"Love you, too, Aunt Lou."

She hung up. I sighed. The frozen veggies shifted a bit in their packaging, thawing, so I paid quickly and left the grocery store with $72 in squashed up bills. The yelling man was gone, and the parking lot was mostly quiet aside from the car alarm going off somewhere in row twelve.

I packed the grocery bags in the backseat of the rental and drove home tired, sweaty and sick to my stomach about how my parents were suddenly making their way onto the California summer landscape. I drove too fast, I know, but I wanted to get back to Alli's, sneak some of her tequila, and get to writing on notecards.

Alli helped me unload the car. I put the food away while she organized the cleaning supplies under the sink. "They didn't have my floor stuff?" she asked.

"If they did, I didn't see it. I saw a homeless man, though. He was yelling and–"

"You didn't give him any money, did you?" Alli's voice was low and coated in concern.

"Nope," I lied.

"Good. We have a real druggie problem here. If they want to rot on heroin so badly, they can get a job and pay for it themselves."

"Right," I said, then retreated to my room with notecards, a pen, and a Spanish-English dictionary from the shelf in the hallway.

* * *

Andrew was not my first kiss. Tyler was. On the last night of the conference, Tyler and I were up late talking about what it's like not being able to describe the American Dream as a teenager. We had our own dreams, and America was nothing more than a landmark.

"I'm not very patriotic," I told him.

"Why not?"

"Because we were born from war," I said. "And when we can't find someone to fight, we go to war with ourselves."

"That's a sad way to look at it."

"How else?"

"Hmmm...like a constant struggle for peace."

I put my chin in my hands and moped, looking Tyler in the eyes.

"You good?" he asked.

"Not really."

"Why not?"

"Because the whole world wants to kill itself for peace."

"But there's peace during war, still, and I think that's great."

"How so?"

"Even during war, people can kiss each other."

That made me smile, so I confessed to Tyler that I had never kissed another guy before. "Let's fix that right now," he said, then gave me a quick kiss on the lips. "How's that?"

"Peaceful," I said.

We kept in touch after the conference – until the night of the broken laptop – and we even went as far as sending each other little gifts in the mail. Kelly let me use her mailing address so my parents wouldn't find out, and it was through her mailing address that I sent a letter telling Tyler that I wouldn't be able to talk anymore. I made sure to emphasize how finite the decision was and told him not to write back. After Kelly told me the letter was officially sent off, I threw away the things he sent me, including a handmade trinket with his thumbprint on it. In his letter, Tyler said it represented how the things we love are unique to ourselves, like a fingerprint. My time with Tyler was short, but he showed me how to create pockets of peace in a life filled with metaphorical war.

Andrew woke up to find me in the living room of his apartment taping the last label to the lamp in the corner. I woke up early and was quiet enough that I could get most of the note cards put up before Andrew's alarm went off. It took one whole roll of tape and most of a second just to label the furniture, appliances, utensils, and rooms with their Spanish names.

"What's all this?" he asked, wearing an expression of awe that I hadn't seen on his face before.

"They're just words," I said, downplaying the hell out of it. They were more than just words, but I wasn't going to let him see that I knew it too. Andrew put his hands on my waist and kissed me on my left-side temple, which caused a ripple of chills across the back of my neck and down my arms.

"Well, that was very sweet of you," Andrew said. "Thank you."

I started to say "it's nothing" but my phone started ringing from the nightstand in the bedroom we shared. It was Carol.

"Hey Carol–"

"Zach quit."

"What?" I asked. She wasn't going to go on unless I pried.

"Yep. Quit this morning. Can you come in?"

I looked over at Andrew, who had no choice but to overhear the high-volume speaker that was Carol. He nodded, smirking, which told me he didn't mind me dropping our plans for an extra shift at the restaurant. I still can't remember what we had planned that day because the fire was that distracting.

The rumors that the disgruntled Zach started the fire were quickly extinguished, as we learned that the fire was instead the consequence of the grease build-up behind the grill. The intense heat ignited the small, grease-coated section of the wall, creating clouds of smoke and flames. It was an accident. But even though it had nothing to do with Zach, my being there that morning to deal with it was entirely his fault.

Sarah and I helped the customers get out of the smoke and out through the back patio toward the parking lot. Only the ones sitting in the front dining room got to leave out through the front doors. Some took pictures as they left, and I thought it was ridiculous. Smoke was the only thing that showed up.

Pat grabbed the fire extinguisher from under the stainless-steel sink, and the fire went out in no time, proving that it was much smaller than we thought it was. I was glad that it was Pat who took the initiative, because I didn't know where the fire extinguisher was and would have thrown the pitcher of iced-tea at the burning wall; something that would have had no effect on greasy flames.

"Son of a bitch," Pat said, smearing smoke and ashes across his forehead. "That's it?"

"Guess so," said the line cook. I hadn't learned his name, but I wasn't sure he knew mine either. It didn't matter. It was hot as hell outside on the patio where all of us waited for the fire department to finish their complementary inspection. Most of the smoke had cleared, but there was a thick, hazy film that coated everyone's perception. No one was hurt, but no one got their tips and that made for a lousy time.

We sat outside for almost an hour before a tall, lanky fireman strolled out of the building. The sun cut through smoke but not through his shadow that seemed to blend with his body and the ground at the same time. I didn't bother learning his name, either. There was dandruff in his goatee.

"It's all clear," he said. "You can host folks again as early as tomorrow, just be sure to cover that hole. We'll run an inspection in a month."

Carol repeated his choppy words into her cellphone to the owners waiting for updates on the other end. The firemen left and we started to mop, sweep, and scrub The Gilded Naupaka. I volunteered to call the ones who had reservations to ask them if they wanted to cancel or reschedule. Most of the people I called were understanding, but there were two who yelled at me through the phone. I was glad there were only six or seven pending reservations in all.

To give myself a way out from doing something boring like wiping down walls, I hid out in the neon alley to call Andrew. At first, he was worried, but when I told him how small the fire actually was, he laughed. He asked if I was staying the rest of the day. I thought about it, but since Zach was only scheduled for the first shift, I decided to leave. Andrew and I met up for lunch downtown, then parted ways for the afternoon. He had work at the hotel, and I had nothing to do but drift in and out of midseason contemplations.

When Alli came home, I was sitting on her cold, leather couch reading a magazine with a glass of tequila and orange juice. I wasn't using a coaster and was worried that Alli would see the ring of dewy condensation my glass left on her coffee table. She was carrying a dress covered in plastic, and I recognized it as a bridesmaid dress. Kayla and her fiancé Dillan were getting married that following week.

"I see you found the tequila," she said. I only smirked. "Not that it was hidden, really." Alli slid the dress into the coat closet by the door. "Did you burn something?"

"No, the restaurant caught fire."

"Oh yeah, that's right."

"'That's right?'" I said, unnerved by her unflinching.

"Yeah, Carol called. Told me not to come in."

"Oh," I said, taking off my reading glasses. "How's Kayla?"

"Kayla is a *mess* right now, but I'm here for her. Not like that bitch, Megan." Alli paused for a moment, shaking her head while she got a glass of orange juice (without tequila). Then she said, "What are you wearing to the wedding?"

"Don't know," I said, then set the magazine on top of the water ring before Alli could see it.

11

Kayla and Dillan had their wedding on a Thursday, of all days. Alli was in the wedding party as "just a bridesmaid" so I had to be there too. We were all crammed into the small hotel courtyard, and all I could think about were the cold drinks sitting in the shade across from the groom's side. When I went for one, Alli told me to help finish setting up the decorations first, which was irritating. Alli complained all week about how much money and time Kayla was wasting by having a ceremony at all. None of this was told to Kayla directly, of course, only to me – the eighteen-year-old who didn't even think marriage was an option for him, let alone an entire ceremony.

The decorations were simple, but not so simple that attention to detail couldn't be appreciated. Alli spent hours that morning making sure it all looked the way Kayla wanted, and not a single table was without its perfectly positioned roses. The gauzy fabric moved in the breeze above us; twisting around the scents of flowers and perfumes.

I stayed near the doors, hoping to catch some of the cool air from inside the hotel, while Kayla's mom – *Ms. Hasegawa* to me – scolded the caterers.

"No no, it's no good," she said. "Can't be four. Has to be seven."

"There won't be enough for the other tables, though."

Ms. Hasegawa thought about it, then said, "Fine. Three is good." The caterer groaned, removed one of the four rolls of bread from the basket then went back inside to repeat the process with the others.

"Why not four?" I asked.

"Four resembles *death*," Ms. Hasegawa said. "Very unlucky. We avoid this number."

"Good to know," I said

"Go sit, go sit," she said, so I went to sit with Andrew. Twenty minutes later, the ceremony started.

Kayla said I could bring a guest, so I brought Andrew. He wore jeans and a light-blue striped shirt. I wore a white button down with blue buttons in an attempt to match. Both of us sweated through our clothes, though, as the San Diego sun cut through the fabric canopy and onto our backs. Alli looked overheated too, but she couldn't slouch in a chair like Andrew and I. Instead, she was stuck standing with the wedding party, fanning herself with the card she "forgot" to put in the box by the entrance. Later, she tried to say she was too busy helping Kayla to remember the card, but I knew she held on to it on purpose because she knew how hot it was going to be. I even caught her staring at the cold drinks more than once, but she straightened up and smiled when she saw me watching her. Like me, she knew when people were keeping tabs.

At one point in the ceremony, the pastor said, "but we must give credit to God for helping these two find each other," and Kayla and Dillan looked at each other like they believed it. It's fine if they believed it, but I didn't. They met each other through an app and only decided to get married because they were religiously impatient people. And even though they had only known each other a year, Ms. Hasegawa was crying so hard she gave herself hiccups.

Dillan and Kayla kissed when prompted, and we, the half-boiled audience, applauded. After the crowd embraced itself in photos and sobs, Andrew and I decided to find ourselves in line for ice cream a few blocks away. I picked cookies and cream, for the texture, but Andrew picked Vanilla and I thought that was so boring. *Vanilla?* I thought. *Even the word is bori–*

"Do your parents know?"

"Know what?"

"That you're gay."

Not wanting to call it what it was, I tried to buy more time by taking a long lick of the cone. It didn't work. "Kinda."

"Kinda?"

In my mind, I saw the snap of a laptop screen and a yet-to-be-paid $283. "It wasn't good."

Andrew nodded, looking over at a gull plucking barnacles off the rocks. "Well, what do you like more, California or Colorado?"

"It's hot here. And I miss the rain. It doesn't rain here."

"It does, sometimes."

We had ice cream, and I thought, for the moment, that was good enough. I didn't need the rain; not that day. "The food's better here, though."

"Oh yeah?"

"Yeah, and the people. But the heat, man, it's too much. My hair is pissing me off." I wiped the sweat from my forehead with my sleeve as ice cream dribbled down my fingers.

"I'll give you a haircut."

"Very funny."

"No, really! I have some clippers at the apartment."

"Okay," I said. Impulse became my drug of choice.

"Do you know what kinda cut you want?"

"At this point, a buzzcut."

And that's what I got, a few hours later, on his balcony. He brought the chair out and faced it away from the setting sun, plugged in some extension cords, and gave me a buzzcut right there while he played music out of a Bluetooth speaker perched on the ledge of the railing. The clippers buzzed against my scalp, and I felt the pieces of my hair fall from my head and onto the bed sheet held behind my neck by a safety pin.

Andrew brushed his hand over the top of my head, and I felt the short hairs of my scalp move under him like wind over prairie grass.

"All done," he said, handing me a small mirror with a cracked handle.

I brushed my own hand over my scalp in long, slow movements as I gazed into the teary, green eyes in the mirror.

"Did I fuck it up?"

"No! No, not at all, Andrew."

"Oh good, because if I–"

"I love it here!" I said, interrupting him on purpose. I wasn't crying about the hair, and he needed to know that. I glanced westward, where the sun used to be, and couldn't remember what it felt like to be alone. "I love it here...and God gets no credit!"

* * *

Old arcades, coffee shops, historic theaters, and second-hand stores – Andrew and I found ourselves in all of it. I loved knowing that there was always something exciting and authentic to discover, and I was glad to discover all of it with Andrew. He knew all the cool spots that people like me wouldn't ever find on their own. One of my favorite adventures was when we thrifted a pair of suits and snuck around a members-only club. No one even knew we were faking it, but how could they? We were who we said we were to careless strangers.

I ended up spending several nights at Andrew's, and I made sure to tell Alli if I wouldn't be home. There was no way to conceal how involved Andrew and I were with each other, but her knowing about it *and* supporting it made running around with him almost effortless.

Sometimes, Andrew surprised me at work and asked to sit in my section just so we could talk. I would say, "I threw a few extra fries on there for you," and he would leave a handwritten poem on his receipt. One time, Carol apologized to and offered to rehire him, but I was proud of Andrew for declining. She felt really bad about letting Andrew go, but he was molded from integrity and wasn't about to throw away his conviction like that. And besides, he loved his new job at the hotel, or at least he told me he did after our trip to the farmer's market. We were at Ocean Beach Pier.

"Oh look," Andrew said, pointing at a map of the United States stuck to a splotchy teal bulletin board. Push pins were scattered and clumped all over the map to answer the question *WHERE ARE YOU FROM?* painted above it. I was distracted by the thin drip of red paint that fell from the "h" while Andrew picked a red pin and pressed into the middle of Oklahoma.

"You're from Oklahoma?" I asked, wondering how I missed that detail after a month of knowing him. "In a way," he said. It was a quick and deliberate answer. "My mom had a VHS of *Oklahoma!* that she watched with me during the tougher times. It was enough to take me out of my own life for a while, and, well, I grew attached to it. You can be from anywhere that feels like home, so, I'm gonna say I'm from Oklahoma."

"Well, I'm *actually* from Colorado," I said, trying not to dwell, and pressed a blue push pin into the map as close to my hometown as I could.

While the sun set, Andrew and I walked down the beach, stopping at a small collection of rocks that jutted out a ways into the ocean. We held hands as we helped each other over the briny landscape of Ocean Beach, scraping our shins but loving it. After a while on the rocks, we made our way back. As soon as our soaked shoes touched the sand again, we went back to the car where we kissed and felt around for a bit. Soon our pants were off and we had each other in our mouths like inverted lollipops.

Going back to his place and having sex was my idea, not Andrew's. He didn't seem nervous about it, but he was certainly cautious; making sure that it was something I really wanted to do with him. I really did.

"You don't feel pressured, do you? I mean, I don't want you to feel like it's somethi–"

"Of course not," I said. Though I hadn't had sex before Andrew, I wasn't a stranger to sensuality and knew my anatomy well enough to get a good fuck out of the summer.

"If you've never 'held' anyone before, I can show you how."

I said, "Show me," and we fell into each other like there was nothing else our bodies were built for. We were safe, free and loved. I can't speak for Andrew, but I had never felt all three at the same time before.

What followed was a montage of moments, and I even surprised myself with the different ways I let my body move with his. The summer seemed to slow completely, but I wasn't thinking about it because all I had to think about was Andrew. He was on me. My eyes, on him. I made him moan.

By the end of it, we were faint under the robust thickness of the air, so we showered together before getting drunk on the balcony.

"It's been nice," I said. "I don't want to leave." I meant it too. I didn't want to go anywhere. I felt insufferably entitled to a life like the one I lived over the summer. On the edge of true adulthood, I could feel myself peeling away from whatever it meant to be an innocent bystander to my own life. I wanted the whole world, I wanted to share it with Andrew, and I wanted to watch every damn sunset from Ocean Beach Pier, but I only had two weeks left for things like that.

* * *

Even with the AC blasting, the inside of Kayla and Dillan's motorhome was unbearably hot. A wedding gift from Dillan's uncle, the motorhome was meant for the two of them to use on some honeymoon getaway. Kayla, obsessed with company, decided to make it a friend trip instead. The idea was to take the three-hour drive to Joshua Tree Lake Campground and spend the night in the desert.

"Cool enough back there?" Alli shouted from the passenger seat.

I said "Yep" in an unenthusiastic sort of way that told Alli all she needed to know about the poor attitude I had developed by three o'clock on a Sunday.

"Okay. If you want, there's drinks in the minifridge."

"Cool," I groaned and made my way over to the stainless steel minifridge tucked under the counter. The grooved vibration from the road made the glass beer bottles chime against each other. I didn't like the taste of beer, but I drank one anyway, just to keep me tolerable, while Dillan and Alli returned to their unilateral chitchat.

"What made you want to be a realtor?" Alli asked, yelling over the wind. Dillan didn't reply, though. He shrugged. That wasn't the only time it happened, either. Though Alli did most of the talking, Dillan rarely gave a verbal answer. Shrugs, nods and even a thumbs up; it was like he was only halfway listening to her.

A bump in the road caused some of the beer to spill onto my shorts, which would have been less frustrating if I wasn't hurling down the road in an 88 degree crucible. I told Alli that I didn't want to go camping, but she made me go with them, claiming that the trip would be a great opportunity to "disconnect" for a bit. She made sure that I didn't bring anything that required a charger (like my mp3 player) aside from my cell phone, which wouldn't get a signal in the desert anyway. So, I brought the book Yaryna gave me and my favorite poem from Andrew to use as a bookmark.

The first few chapters of the book were *very* slow. It might have been the beer and the heat, but I had to reread several lines just to understand what was going on. By the fifth chapter, I had a solid idea of what was happening, but I had no clue as to why Yaryna wanted me to read it.

The main character, Jack, strayed from the group on a hiking trip and got himself lost in the forest. He didn't complain about it because there was no one to complain to, but Jack was completely accepting of his new circumstances, and that bothered me. The part that bothered me the most was in chapter two when Jack got stuck in a rainstorm. Instead of trying to take shelter, the foolish Jack stood in the middle of it, spread out his arms, and yelled. I thought it was ridiculous.

The sun was a quarter of the way to the horizon when we pulled into the parking lot at Joshua Tree. In a voice too loud for anyone's good, Dillan called out "Here!" which woke up Kayla. Alli, who gave up trying to talk with Dillan an hour ago, shoved the magazine she was reading into her backpack and finished off the last bite of her almond chocolate bar.

After securing our campsite, Alli cooked fish filets on the small, red grill while Dillan and Kayla cut up fruit. Alli asked me to set up the folding table and chairs, but I chose to wander the campground instead, and with my book so that I could try to *at least* get past chapter twelve.

Joshua Tree, as far as national parks are concerned, was flat. There was no other word for it, honestly. If it weren't for the ridges of the hills surrounding the campsite, I might have even considered this landscape the edge of the world. I shook my head at that last thought. There was no edge of the world, because if there were, it would be a well-lit attraction like any other wonder, and people would only go see it just to say they did.

The sun was glaring at me by that point, and the land was so wide that I was as two-dimensional as my own shadow. I figured dinner would take around forty minutes to cook (as long as Alli didn't try to take over), so I walked in the direction of the sun.

While I poked around the campground, I came up with theories about the end of summer. I was sure that my parents would be happy to see me again, but I couldn't tell if I was homesick or not. There was a tradeoff that had to happen, and I wasn't all that thrilled about it because it meant that a version of myself – the version I realized was the *real* me – would have to stay behind in California. I didn't know if I would miss California specifically, but I knew I would miss the proud-self prerogative. Not being able to see Andrew anymore was part of it for sure, but that wasn't the only thing. I had a lot to be happy about, and none of it could fit in a carry-on.

The sun splayed across the earth when I chose to join it on a warm rock. I set the book down next to me, drew in my knees, and turned my head to stare back at the brilliant star that was too far into the horizon to hurt my eyes. I didn't rush. I didn't even *think* about rushing. The sun set, I let out a sigh, and that was the end of it.

Back at the motorhome, the food was covered with towels and the drinks were coated in droplets of condensed desert rays. Alli said, "Oh *there* he is," in the tone of passive nonchalance that was uniquely her own. She was slouched against the side of the motorhome while Kayla sat on the ground across from her. I didn't see Dillan.

"You could have started eating," I said.

Kayla, who was drawing lines in the sand with her finger, said, "It's fine, we don't mind. Did you see anything cool out there?"

"Not really. Where's Dillan?"

"Getting the firewood from inside."

"We can have fires here?"

"Don't know," Alli said. "But we'll start it and put it out if we have to. I don't think anyone will say anything, though."

The door of the motorhome swung open and Dillan shifted down the stairs holding a stack of splintered logs. "Need help?" Alli asked, but he didn't reply, which I thought was as annoying as it was rude. It was as if Dillan only replied when he felt like it, but Kayla and Alli didn't seem to mind.

Taking full advantage of the "self-assured" version of myself, I decided to say something to Dillan. "Why don't you answer her?" I asked.

Alli said, "Relax, Ian," but I didn't. My confidence evolved into shouting.

"Alli asked if you needed help, and you ignored her! I know you heard her!"

Dillan's entire body shifted. His shoulders dropped. He bit his upper lip with his bottom teeth and dropped the pile of wood. Alli grabbed my arm.

"Really, Ian!?"

I turned and faced my cousin. "What do you mean 'really'? Don't you think it's rude to-"

"I didn't." Dillan said.

"You didn't *what?*" I said.

Alli's eyebrow hinged upward. She shook her head slowly while I turned back toward Dillan.

"I didn't hear Alli ask anything. I can't always...I'm mostly deaf. Both ears."

Silence banked on the desert. There was nothing else for Dillan to say, but I was tying words into knots with my tongue. I may have started to say a dozen possible things, but each time I tried to speak, only small, glottal chirps came out.

Kayla rose up from the sand. "Let's eat." The other two nodded, glanced at me, and joined Kayla by the food. I was too chastened by embarrassment to hang out, so I drifted up the motorhome steps, kicking up sand from my dusty shoes, and flopped down on the sticky vinyl couch.

I stayed in the camper long enough to feel the heat of the desert sizzle out and cool under the night. There was a leftover orange on the counter, which I ate while trying to listen to the conversations outside. Through the thick walls, I could only pick up on a few sentences now and then. I heard my name, but only twice, and when I heard Alli mention the name of her favorite downtown bookstore, I felt the sharp pang of realization that I accidentally left the book Yaryna gave me propped up on a rock in the desert. I finished the orange in anger.

Soon, stacking pieces of orange peel became my pastime. I shredded them even smaller to see how high the stack could go, but six dime-sized pieces seemed to be the record. I attempted an all-peel model of the Eiffel Tower, and it would have turned out great if I didn't give up on it. After settling on what to say to Dillan, I made a few portraits out of the peel, then threw it away. The room smelled like simmered citrus.

When I finally decided to re-emerge from the motorhome, it wasn't because I got bored with orange pieces. No, it was because I heard Dillan singing. He had a great voice that was unique to him only, and I was nothing but wrong about him. I walked slowly down the steps then maneuvered over to the spot behind Alli. Dillan saw me and stopped singing. Kayla stopped playing and Alli set her drink down.

"Sorry," I said.

Dillan drew an awkward smirk. "It's okay."

"It's not, though...I'm sorry."

Dillan nodded. I nodded back. Kayla started playing the guitar again while I got myself a plate of food. While she played, Dillan and Alli sang along, and I stared down into the fire to watch the glow of the embers brush against the shadows and flame.

Kayla played on even as the coals died, revealing the stars. Without the lights of the city or the fire, the expansivity of the universe was revealed and we saw the bioluminescent sky dance around its own bright miles. We had been at the edge of the world the whole time. It was always above us.

12

"Oh my god, where the hell did your hair go!?" was the first thing my mom said to me when I greeted my parents at LAX. The breeze spilled over the pavement and smelled like tar, which had Alli in a coughing fit. As a consequence of Aunt Lou's coercion, my parents decided to turn my last week in California into a family reunion.

"I cut it," I said, trying not to make a big deal about it. She shook her head.

"But you looked so handsome with it longer."

"It'll grow back," my dad said. He gave me a few pats on my shoulder; the extent of his affection. If he was capable of more than that, I wouldn't know. "I think it looks fine."

My mom threw a stern look at him, then turned back to me with the same expression. "Don't cut it that short again."

I rolled my eyes. "I think it looks fine too, Dad, thanks."

"I guess I can't tell you what to do anymore." This, of course, was not true. In fact, all this statement did was instill guilt, calling back to a time when I was young enough to take everything my parents told me as the only truth in a world built on lies. It wouldn't be until years later that I would discover how mistaken I was to believe that.

"But," my mom pouted. "Look where my advice has gotten you."

I nodded, but not because I agreed. I was pissed that I drove two hours to pick my parents up at the airport only to be insulted about my hair. I put my frustration aside, though, and focused instead on making sure my parents enjoyed their time. Besides, they were happy to see me, and that meant a lot to someone who walked the line between loved and disregarded as often as I did.

L.A. was flashy, and I immediately understood why Alli chose to live two hours south in San Diego. Alli's mom – *Aunt Lou* to me – stayed in L.A. and found herself beachside with her father following their parents' divorce. My dad – *Uncle Jerry* to Alli – left for Colorado to be with his mom. My grandfather's second wife died a few years after, leaving the dynastic L.A. beach house and a large inheritance to the daughter she never had, Aunt Lou.

My parents were already whispering to each other their assumptions and reservations about her and being apart from Aunt Lou gave them a lot of time to come up with self-fabricated reasons for things. The strange thing about it all was that even though my parents made a considerable amount of money and could afford to live on the beach too if that's what they wanted, there was a current of jealousy that flowed between the two of them. I think it's because Aunt Lou didn't have to do more than take care of my grandpa; do his shopping, drive him to appointments, and finally, plan for his burial – all of which was much more than my dad did for my grandma. No, my dad made special arrangements for assisted living, and my grandma died in the middle of the night with no one there but the nurse who found her rigid in the morning. But even after all that, my mom and dad had something to say about Aunt Lou getting everything handed to her.

The four of us arrived at the beach house, and Aunt Lou was outside waiting for us. I had not seen Aunt Lou in several years and saw the ways that aging had affected her. Her wavy, brunette hair had been replaced by silver, and the shoulders that used to stand proudly back dipped forward. Her smile was the same, though, and it proved that she was honored to see us again. I looked over at my parents and they seemed happy too.

Aunt Lou helped us in with our bags and started showing off all the recently finished renovations she had done to the house. Aunt Lou lived alone and was a very capable person who did not believe in paying other people for work that could be done on one's own.

Unlike my parents, though, I had nothing to compare the renovations to, because, until that morning, I had never seen the house. For family gatherings in the past, Aunt Lou always made the trip to Colorado.

My parents have seen the house twice, though, to my knowledge. One time to help Aunt Lou clean it out before moving in, and a second time on an anniversary trip my parents took years prior. It felt strange to walk through a house that I had never seen but heard so much about.

"Your rooms are upstairs, kids," Aunt Lou said while handing Alli and I each a towel and a washcloth.

Alli laughed and said "'Kids?'"

"Hey, lose the attitude, missy, and show Ian where his room is." Aunt Lou kissed Alli's cheek and gave her a light squeeze around her shoulders. Alli returned the cheek kiss and started up the stairs. I followed.

On the wall along the stairs was an immense collection of photographs of our family. I recognized cousins, grandparents, and a handful of others that I had only met once or twice but couldn't remember the names of. I saw Alli's school pictures that were placed chronologically by year. There were photos of myself as a kid, and some old family photos that my dad must have sent years ago.

At the top of the stairs was a larger photo. My parents had a smaller print of it in their living room. It was of my dad and Aunt Lou standing behind their parents. My grandmother's hands were placed delicately on her lap; my grandfather's hand on her knee and his other in his pocket.

"Here's your room," Alli said. I didn't notice that she had already made her way down the hall.

"Thanks."

"Mine's over here." She cleared her throat. In her eyes I saw the glossy indication of tears. She was much closer to grandma than I was and knew that this was not something I could relate to, as far as real emotions are concerned. At that point in my life, I had not experienced what it felt like to lose someone I *cared* about. When my grandfather died, I didn't even try to understand what was happening. I didn't notice any change in myself, only that I wasn't sad. I only met him twice, so how could I have been? What I did notice, however, was how the family dynamics changed in the years that followed. It was after his death that my dad and his sister stopped contacting each other, and only called on holidays or birthdays. Lou stopped flying out to Colorado to visit and Alli and I only reconnected because she wanted to invite us all to her high school graduation. My parents told her that we couldn't make it, but Alli and I touched base once or twice a year after that.

We all sat at what would be our usual spots at the dinner table. My dad cleared the dishes – something he only did at other people's houses. After dinner, I wanted to go right to my room, but my mom stopped me at the bottom of the stairs.

"Hey," she said, "Your dad and I were talking, and we think that next year, you might want to help Carlos out at the funeral home."

"And why would I want to do that?" I asked.

"Because he's old, Ian. It's the right thing to do."

"Well, maybe I–"

"Besides," she cut me off, "it's better than being a *waiter*. You're so above that."

"I don't want to bury people," I said.

"He needs help, Ian."

"What about Robin?"

"Robin only just started."

"I'll think about it," I told her, then turned quickly up the stairs. In the room, I set my bag down by the dresser, kicked off my shoes, and flopped onto the bed with a sigh. I was careful not to smile too loudly while I texted Andrew to tell him I missed him.

He texted back, "miss you too, my lemon," which gave me a very loud smile indeed.

* * *

At breakfast, Aunt Lou handed each of us an aquarium ticket. "They're day passes," she said, "So we don't have to rush!" Not rushing through an aquarium sounded like the best way for all of us to get out of each other's ways, so I was on board. Also, I had only been to an aquarium once before, during a school trip. I enjoyed the visit, though, and was enthralled by the strange species that Colorado could never support.

"Thanks Aunt Lou!" I said and stacked our breakfast dishes in a pile. Alli grabbed everyone's napkins for the laundry. Aunt Lou had a habit of stealing napkins from her travels as souvenirs, so none of the napkins matched.

I put a few pieces of candy in my pocket, grabbed my mp3 player, and followed my family to the car, thrilled to be going to an aquarium and not a tourist trap designed for Hollywood headaches. And since Aunt Lou bought the tickets way ahead of time, we were able to walk past the line at the front and go right inside where people moved in currents.

"Let's all meet back here at four and see how we feel after that," Alli said, and the five of us split up. Alli and Aunt Lou together, my mom with my dad, and me on my own but happy about it.

I wandered through the deep-sea exhibit first, which was mostly made up of a collection of interactive models and life-size recreations of the things that live too far away from the sun's influence. I didn't spend a lot of time there and instead found myself at the tide pools where a red octopus in a cylindrical tank greeted me. It gripped the walls with a few of its arms while the others twisted and rolled around each other; feeling the ridges of rock and kelp. A large, unblinking eye faced me, but I couldn't tell if it was looking at me, specifically, or at the vastness of the world of humans behind me. I think it saw me, though, and recognized me as an individual entity separate from my environment, just as I saw the octopus separate from its own world. Yes, I'm sure of it. It was just the two of us staring into the eye of the other.

What's your opinion of me? I thought, surprised by the strangeness of my sudden existentialism. Its eyes shifted downward, just a millimeter, then back up. Its red arms were mostly motionless, but now and then the octopus would uncurl one as it felt around the rock. I shook my way out of that headspace and left the all-knowing octopus alone.

The waist-high tanks of tide pool creatures bubbled and glistened under the natural light of the sun coming in through the westward windows. A few employees circled through; their minds full of facts about spiny urchins and anemone potency. An urchin was offered up to me, but I didn't want to touch it. Something about touching it felt invasive, and I didn't want to make enemies with tide pool creatures. After about thirty minutes, I went to the entrance of the room, back toward the eight-armed sentinel. I noticed, though, that while I was distracting myself with tide pools, an additional tank had been wheeled in.

The tank wasn't very large and fit perfectly on the small rolling table. There was some sand at the bottom of the tank, but the environment was not set up like the others. It was a temporary home.

Like the tide pools, an employee dressed in a blue t-shirt stood proudly by the tank. The words "CAN YOU GUESS MY AGE?" bounced off the bold, fluorescent paper glued to a wooden skewer protruding from the sand. Curious, I approached the tank as a clawless lobster crawled out from the murk.

"This is Jerry!"

Startled, I glanced up at the insistent one.

"Jerry is a spiny lobster, which is a native species to our warm California waters! We found Jerry right on the other side of the pier." Here, she took a breath and gestured grandly toward the undoubtedly oblivious lobster.

"That's my dad's name."

"I'm sorry?"

"Jerry. That's my dad's name. Short for Jeremiah."

The lobster-sitter forced a laugh. "That's so funny! Well, today is *this* Jerry's last day with us at the aquarium. He's been a big help to our experts tracking the population of spiny lobsters in the area. When the aquarium closes, a small group of experts will release him back into the wild!"

"Where are his claws?" I asked, suddenly concerned with the abnormalities of lobsters.

"Oh, spiny lobsters don't have claws, actually." I hated the way she said "actually" as if I was supposed to know that California spiny lobsters are born without claws. "Our biologists were able to determine how old Jerry is. Would you like to take a guess? We're giving away two free aquarium tickets to whoever guesses correctly!" Her short, curly blonde hair bounced as if she was animated by one of Walt's crew.

"Sure," I said, taking a pen and a pink slip of paper from off the table. I stared down at the lobster in the tank while I tried to come up with some reasonable guess. I had heard before that lobsters can live up to a hundred years, or close to a hundred years at least, but I didn't know what an "old" lobster looked like. I noticed the small crowd waiting in line behind me, and since I was already taking too long to guess how old a lobster was, I wrote down the only number I associated with a lobster – a golden VII.

I jotted down "7" and didn't even bother putting a line through it like I usually do when I write my sevens. The paper fell gently into the cardboard box and landed softly inside, but I couldn't tell by the sound how many other guesses there were. It was a nice thought, though, taking Andrew to the aquarium, just us two.

"You're in a group, Ian, act like it," my dad scorned when I finally rejoined the group. It was 4:17.

"Who's hungry?" Aunt Lou threw in, no doubt sensing the tension. The group agreed that we were all hungry, so we filed out of the aquarium and made our way to some seafood joint a little way down the block. Aunt Lou wanted to keep the day in theme, which from what I remembered from childhood, was Aunt Lou's whole deal.

The wait for a table was twenty minutes, which my dad blamed me for, since I kept everyone waiting. I knew he would offer to pay for everyone's meal, so I threw mine up in the restaurant bathroom. My dad hated wasting money and I hated being blamed for things.

While I unwrapped the red and white peppermint from my pocket, I realized how long it had been since I last made myself throw up. Something that used to be so routine for me suddenly felt foreign. I wasn't ashamed or guilty for doing it, but I didn't recognize it in myself as something I did anymore. I wondered how many other habits had dissolved away since I got to California. I washed my hands and left my contemplations in the bathroom mirror where they belonged.

Later that night, while Alli and Aunt Lou were out shopping, my parents tried to talk to me about the funeral home again, but I avoided it by going upstairs to take a shower. I left my phone on the breakfast bar to charge, next to my aquarium ticket, ID, and debit card, all in a neat little pile. When I got out of the shower, my mom, breathy and sobbish, called my name from the kitchen.

"Yeah?" I hollered down the stairs.

My dad's voice replied, "We...we need to talk when you're done."

"Um, okay," I said, and took my time getting dressed. My teeth were chattering and I hated that. My mind spiraled down every avenue of bizarre reasons for why I could be in trouble. I stopped stalling, put on my clothes, and decided to get it over with.

I made my way down the stairs, passing all of the photos and portraits, and emerged at the entrance of the kitchen to find my dad leaning against the sink, my mom with her head in her hands, and my phone, open and glowing on the countertop between them. I took a sharp breath as my gut dropped.

My mom lifted her head from her palms and turned to me, her makeup boiling on her red-flushed face. "Who the hell is Andrew?"

13

"Just a friend from work!" I repeated, shouting. I felt the blood in my ears pound against the cartilage. She didn't believe me, having heard this lie several times before from her husband, the patron saint of infidelity.

"Don't fucking lie, Ian! I *hate* liars!" My mom slammed my phone down on the counter, and I flinched. My dad didn't move at all and stayed staring at me from the other side of the kitchen.

"We read the messages," he said.

I said nothing while my teeth chattered.

"Well?" he said, trying to guilt a confession out of me.

"I thought we talked about this!" my mom blurted. "You said – you *promised* us – that you weren't gay." Her eyes bounced slightly back and forth as she scanned my face for any sort of reason or answer to the questions in her mind, but I stayed quiet. I looked over at my dad. His eyes were fixed on a spot on the wall.

"You are so goddamn selfish," my dad said. "We do *so much* for you, Ian."

"I don't get it. I just don't."

"Did you have sex?"

Deep breath. Shaky. Shifting position and burning eyes.

"No, no of course not," I lied, but at least I was finally speaking. Pried open and raw in front of an audience of weeping parents. They sighed, relieved, and I did too – relieved that I was a good enough liar for them to believe even that much of it. I felt like I was drowning in lies and accusations just because Andrew melted my wax and feather wings.

"Thank God," my dad said.

They both stared at me, waiting for me to say something, but I was not going to let them get any closer to meeting the person I became in California. I really thought I had them on the retreat, too, because they both looked so scared of me. Ashamed of me, yes, but scared too. Scared that some shadowy thing lived in me and wanted to rip into our family's heartstrings when all it was the part of me that needed love. I hoped for words, but the words did not exist because I couldn't let them.

My dad lumbered across the tile floor. After four heavy steps, he stood directly in front of me and put his hands imperiously on my shoulders. "If this, or any form of this, comes up again, your mother and I would no longer consider you our son."

"What!?"

"You heard him!" my mom said. The air snapped. "You won't be welcome in our home, and you'll have to figure shit out on your own."

As I stared wide-eyed at the damp face of my mother, I heard the gravel of Aunt Lou's driveway shift and grind under the tires of her car. My parents heard it too.

"We're done," my mom said, and immediately wiped her face dry.

My dad cleared his throat and slid my phone to me. "No more talking to Andrew," he said, and it was somehow over.

I took the phone, went upstairs, climbed into bed, and counted breaths between fever dreams. Eighteen years of love and upbringing hinged on the next lie I told. My life, my future, my everything depended on something so fragile as an eighteen-year old's ability to play a series of roles for other people. There was no way the "Lemon" I was in California could survive in Colorado, and I knew that. I sacrificed my own soul just so it could be saved in the eyes of my parents.

* * *

The next morning, my parents and I hardly spoke to each other. We kept up our "normal" attitudes in front of Alli and Aunt Lou, but only because my mom and dad would have lost it if anyone saw us acting any other way. I heard Alli ask about me, but my mom told her I wasn't feeling well. I guess she wasn't wrong, but it was still misleading. I was wracked from the night before and was careful to not make anything worse before they flew back to Colorado that afternoon. I offered to carry their things to Lou's car – she volunteered to drive them – and my dad followed me out.

"I called Carlos earlier this morning and told him you would be ready for work when you get back."

I shut the hatch, stunned. "Wait, what do you–"

"Besides," he continued, silencing me. "It's a real job; not like this waiter crap."

"I don't want to work at a funeral home." I protested. At this, my mom came out, carrying a plastic bag of seashells.

"He was very excited to hear it," she said, setting the shells down on the floor of the front passenger side. "Now give us a hug, we're leaving."

The request of sentiment took all meaning out of it. I said, "I love you," and they replied "Love you too," in a stern, unfeeling way that solidified my guilt and inability to protest. The two of them got in the car and waited there until Aunt Lou was ready. When I went back inside, I ran shoulder-first into Aunt Lou, who I didn't see coming down the hallway. The jarring action made us both stop, and she saw in one pass how lost I was.

"Give me a hand in the kitchen," she said and kept walking. Her words were quick but not unkind. I leaned against the doorframe of the kitchen while Aunt Lou wiped the counter with a dish towel.

"Everything ok?" she asked, flopping the towel into the sink.

"Yeah, why?"

"You can tell me if it's not, Ian. I've known enough people to recognize a troubled mind." I didn't look at her, which was enough to tell her what was up. "Your parents, they...they want the best for you and–"

"I know."

"I'm going to tell you something, Ian, about people. So don't interrupt."

She tilted her forehead toward me and glanced at me from over the top of her glasses. I nodded, and leaned back against the soggy countertop; resting my palms on the surface.

"When I got this house, your dad called me and told me how selfish I was. He told me every way left and right that it was wrong to accept it, or that I didn't deserve it or whatever it was, it didn't matter. He had something to say, fine, I get it. I didn't get it then, but I do now. I mean, it was our dad for fuck's sake. Anyway, this is where we grew up. Not here in this house but here in this part of town – on the coast – and he left to follow our mom, which is fine, but he thought he could tell me how I, in his mind, should live. But I chose to *stay* and that was good enough for me. Your parents, no, your dad chose to leave. I chose to stay."

Even if I thought I had a lot to say, I didn't say anything at all. I just listened to that long moment of silence as she looked at me.

"You have to choose, Ian, the places in the world you want to be a part of because you can't have all of it. That's what makes us who we are, like it or not."

I nodded. She stepped out of the kitchen and left me alone with the last word. After my parents left for the airport, Alli and I drove back down to San Diego.

Andrew asked to meet me at the pier as soon as I made it back. That's what his text said, at least, and that he had a gift for me. I didn't reply, not at first, but after a while I texted an unfeeling "sure" and set my phone in the cupholder. My flight back to Colorado was the next afternoon, and my mind was in a stalemate of conflictions. I couldn't have been any more numb. I had nothing to myself but the guilt created by loving parents. In my mind, that guilt, the *poison* of that disappointment, was more powerful than whatever love I found in a summer. Alli could tell that I wasn't handling any of myself well.

"I can come back in a bit if you wan–"

"No," I said, coldly. "I'll be quick."

"You sure? Because if–"

"Alli, I said I'll be quick." I spoke in bold whispers. Sharp.

Alli parked off to the side and let me out a short way from the pier. Andrew was leaning on the rail, lost in the mix of his own thoughts and the scene around him. He hadn't noticed me yet, but I couldn't stand to look anywhere else than at him. I cleared my throat so I wouldn't cry, but I was apprehensive and there was no hiding that. He would know. I was reckless in loving him, and that made me an enemy of truth. Sorrow ran putrid in my bloodstream and pounded itself against my jaw. I walked too fast.

"Andrew!" I called. He turned, pushed himself away from the rail, and met me halfway to the shore. I drifted into him with a hug, hiding my face in his neck. I looked up at him and we kissed. I was hurt and he knew it.

"Hey, is everything alright?" he asked.

"Yeah, I'm just tired." A lie.

"I'll make it quick so you and Alli can go and rest, but I wanted to ask you something." I could tell he was nervous. Actually, it was the first time all summer that I saw this nervous side of him. The truth.

"I know you're leaving tomorrow, but..." He cleared his throat, then, "Oh, you know what? This first." He reached into his jacket pocket and pulled out a golden tennis bracelet with little jewels embedded in each segment. The sun caught the angle of the jewels and it was beautiful. "This is for you."

He placed his left hand under my right, and set a gleaming, hand-polished bracelet into my palm. I held it tightly between my fingers as I lifted it closer to the sun; closing one eye as I did so that I could observe the fractals of the gems more closely.

"They're not real," Andrew said, shoving his hands deep into his pockets.

"What?"

"The diamonds. They're fake."

"They don't need to be real, it's beautiful. Thank you."

"I found it at a thrift shop, but something told me to get it for you. I was wandering around the store when I noticed a man leaning over the jewelry case. He closed his eyes and pressed his face to the glass. Then he started to cry. Not out loud, but there was a tear left on the glass after he left. I know, because I wanted to see what he was looking at. It was a locket, propped open, and I saw in it the photo of the man and a woman. I think someone he knew used to wear it, but they didn't take the picture out. Next to it was the bracelet, so I bought it. When I got to the counter, I asked if the cashier knew if the diamonds were real or not and she laughed. 'Would they be in a place like this if they were?' she asked me, and I thought to myself, 'Well I'm here, and I'm real. That man and his love were real, and both of them were here, so yes.' Then she told me that they were cubic zirconia, so it's a fake. But still nice, I think."

I held up my wrist, and Andrew helped me put it on. I looked out at the seascape. There was a bottle of wine propped up securely in the sand. My conscience was at war with heartbeats.

"Ian," he said, pulling my gaze away from the coast and into his kind, hazel eyes. "Will you stay?"

"What?"

"Will you stay here with me in California?"

"Andrew."

"Look, I know it sounds crazy, but..." He looked down at the discarded shells of the summer that were strewn about our feet. "We can make it work. There's a great college here, and you already have a job, and—"

As he spoke, I could tell that the longer I took to reply, the more alone in the idea he felt. His words trailed off. He got quiet. There was pain in his eyes that matched the pain in mine. It was still for a moment, as the sea lapped at the shore, then an ardent "I love you, Ian" sailed from his lips, and that hurt both of us.

Tears sat on the edges of my eyelids, but I did not let them fall. I refused. What's worse, I lied.

"I can't. I don't feel the same way."

Andrew held on for a moment before letting his demeanor shift. He picked up his head and looked out at the rocks, then at the ground, then out at the rocks again. When he took a step back, I could tell that, unlike me, he let his tears fall.

"Andrew, I—"

"Thanks for being honest with me, Lemon." He nodded and turned away.

"Here," I said, fidgeting with the clasp of the bracelet. "You should—"

"Nah, keep it. It's a gift," he said, not turning back. "Thanks for a fun summer."

I expected him to argue, to call me out or curse. But he didn't. He accepted my lie as a truth because he was just that good of a person. I stood like a fool as the man I loved made his way down the beach. His silhouette grew smaller and smaller until I couldn't distinguish him from the other beachgoers. I walked back to the car breathless and cold, and left my better judgment and a bottle of wine on the beach behind me.

"What's wrong?" Alli asked. I slammed the car door, half intentionally, half by accident.

"Nothing," I said. "But I gotta pack, so let's go."

Back at Alli's place, I closed myself up in my room and wilted with the day. I turned the bracelet over in the dim light. I unclasped and clasped it again, over and over, and in the tiny jewels I saw the many, miniature reflections of myself. Each face seemed different than the one next to it, even if they were all supposed to be me. And just like the jewels, I was an authentic recreation of myself. Yaryna was right. I was a real fake.

Around four, Alli came to check on me, but I didn't let her in on how I was feeling. She said something about lunch the next day – one last adventure before I flew out – but I wasn't really listening. She went to bed a few hours later, and by eleven I still wasn't sleeping.

I put my headphones in like I do whenever I think too loudly, grabbed a bottle of Alli's tequila, and snuck out through the bedroom window.

* * *

Before landing face-down on the sidewalk, I was convinced that not only was I going to die quickly, but that *I* would be the reason for it and *not* the car. I had just taken a very long shower, my laptop was in pieces on my bedroom floor, and my parents had gone to bed. I was seventeen years old, running to the highway in the middle of a spring rainstorm with the goal of jumping out in front of the fastest car on the road.

I chose to take Cedar Avenue to avoid Kelly's house, but Cedar Avenue was uphill from my parents' home, and the rain had soaked the pavement making it slick. My worn-out shoes had no traction and I fell hard on the sidewalk. I didn't make it to the highway. I didn't even make it three blocks.

One. One, two, th- one.... two, three...one, two.

Trying not to pass out by counting raindrops was hopeless, but my breath came back shortly after, so I relied on that instead. The rain was so loud, made worse by having hit the side of my head on the sidewalk. Most of the pain was in my chin, though. It wasn't in me to sit up right away. I didn't have the strength for it, which made me realize I didn't have the strength to die. I rested my forehead on the concrete and sobbed while blood from my chin was rinsed away by the storm.

My parents didn't hear me come in, but I was glad about that. I was soaked and alone, but I needed to be at that moment. In silence, I picked up the pieces of the laptop and threw it away while thinking about how something in the rain wanted me to live even if I didn't.

How could I not think about that rainy night while I drifted through streets and avenues in North Park drunk on Alli's tequila? The streets echoed my footsteps and the neon signs in bar windows called through the dark. I couldn't see where the moon was.

I was walking along a brick wall that surrounded some storage units when two guys approached me asking, no, *demanding* money. They were not victims of homelessness, as far as I could tell from their clean faces and bright jewelry. They were stray dogs, but not stray like me. I was sure the diamonds in the taller guy's earrings were real.

"I don't have money," I said. My left shoulder went numb as I was thrust into the brick.

"Don't fuck with us," he said.

"I said I don't–" My nose cracked, and I smelled copper. One of them forced me to the ground while the other dug through my pockets searching for whatever credit cards or cash I didn't have on me because I didn't carry a wallet. When they discovered that all I had was a lousy mp3 player and a shitty phone, they kicked me a few times and left with a half-empty bottle of homemade tequila. I didn't even try to fight back because I was alone, eighteen, and over it.

I stood up and fell against the brick wall. My jaw hurt like hell, and I had almost no feeling in my right arm. I couldn't flex my fingers and my leg was sore after the kick to my thigh. I ambled down the sidewalk dripping blood and wishing over and over that they kicked me just a little harder in the back of my head and killed me. I was just another shape in the dark hiding from streetlights. After a few blocks I found a little gas station

– the brightest damn light I could find – and crumpled to the curb.

I used the sleeve of my hoodie to clean up the blood around my face, but it seemed pointless. Blots dripped out from the red rivers inside me. I couldn't stop the bleeding, so I accepted that there was no way I was going to make it back to Alli's unless I called her. She was there in twenty minutes.

In my last moment of consciousness, I whispered "Thanks, dog catcher," and passed out bloody and sore on the pavement. My body was outlined in the glow of gas station lights while my blood pooled with gasoline.

* * *

I didn't remember passing out. I didn't remember waking up, either, but I know it happened because I was propped up in a hospital bed with an IV and the company of Alli, a nurse, and a police officer. And since I had no idea what happens to near-to-death eighteen-year-olds who pass out from tequila and mugging, Alli filled me in on *all* the hard-to-miss details. Specifically, details about how I threw up in the car, I had a concussion, fractured elbow, and broken jaw, and that I was *almost* issued a Minor in Possession by the cop at the end of the bed. Oh, and that I said, "Which one?" when the nurse asked me what my name was.

"Man, you were *out of it*," Alli said.

"I guess," I said while the cop made his way to my left side. The tender muscles around my neck burned as I turned to face him, and Alli took a seat in the chair by the window. I think his name was Officer Kenwold, but I can't remember because his name tag was hiding under a pair of *really cool* sunglasses that reminded me of salted caramel. Officer Somethingwold explained that by the time they were able to get a sample, most of the liquor was out of my system, and since I didn't have any liquor in my possession, they couldn't give me an MIP.

At the end of his spiel, he said, "You think about that next time."

"Sure," I said, and the cop nodded, convinced he had achieved due diligence status in hero points.

Alli stood up and shook his hand, thanked him again for his help, and was careful enough to shut the door gently behind him. "You sure you still want to fly out today? We can change the flight."

"Yeah," I said. "I need to get home."

Since a broken jaw was the worst of it, I was safe to fly. Alli and I were mostly silent for the rest of the morning, and I was overwhelmed by the number of silent conversations I was having with the people I loved.

After leaving the hospital, we had about twenty minutes in the car to say anything at all, but we didn't. It wasn't until I had my backpack and teal suitcase stacked by the door that I gave a weak, "Thanks, sorry."

"It's fine, Ian," Alli said, trying her best to laugh it off. She knew how embarrassed I was. "Oh, wait hold on a sec."

She jogged through the living room into the kitchen. I waited while she dug through her purse on the counter, then pulled out an unopened pack of playing cards – the same deck we all played Hearts with during the slow times. Alli, me, and Andrew...all of us, now changed in ways we couldn't know yet.

"Sorry I didn't wrap it."

"Thanks, Alli, they're great."

"Great," she said, and gave me a hug. It was the kind of hug you give someone when you don't think you'll see them again for a while. "You about ready then?" she asked, and I nodded. I hugged Alli and told her I loved her. She replied, "I love you too, Ian," and wiped a tear from under her aviators. I didn't tell Alli how sad I was, though, and I didn't even start tearing up until after I waved goodbye from the window of the airplane.

I left California with a good amount of money, an almost-MIP, and a tennis bracelet made with fake diamonds. I checked my phone. No texts. I knew it was pointless to hope for one. As a last-ditch effort, I texted "sorry" to Andrew, turned off my phone and threw it into my backpack. I was too tired to care where it landed.

As the plane left the airport, I stared down at the coast. It grew smaller and more and more unattainable, and the reality I created for myself began to settle in. The plane turned away from the city and I watched out the window as San Diego sank below the clouds and the sea returned to its place in my imagination.

When the plane landed in Denver, the heavy rain against the beast's metal frame made listening to the flight attendant difficult. I'd gotten off a plane before so I didn't think it mattered, really. Besides, I preferred to hear the rain over another voice telling me what to do.

I thought of Andrew standing on his balcony watching the sun starting to dip into the horizon, whispering "come home," through the time zones. I was angry about how casually everything happened. One event went right into the other as a broken family led to a broken heart, followed by a broken jaw. Simple. And only the people involved could say what happened, because the rest of the world went on without even noticing.

I turned on my phone. There were no texts, only one missed call and a voice message – both from a number I didn't recognize. I pressed the phone to my ear.

It was a short message left by a spirited voice calling to inform me that I had won two free tickets to the aquarium for correctly guessing the age of a lobster.

14

"Where'd that come from?" my dad said, pointing to the tennis bracelet. I had been wearing it for days, but he only noticed it that morning.

"Found it," I said.

"You shouldn't wear it."

"Why not?"

"Looks like a women's bracelet," he said, then left the room. I was seated in my favorite chair in the living room of my parents' house with a stack of papers on my lap to sort through. My mom was on the couch by the front window flipping through a gardening catalog. The fall semester was starting that week, so I had test scores, admission paperwork, and financial statements to submit by Friday. It was Wednesday.

There was no chance of a gap year, so I signed up for an online degree program in English Language Arts. It was nothing exciting, but I knew I could finish in a couple of years while I waited for anything more inspiring. Besides, I caved on the whole funeral home thing, and that was already a lot to manage. Online classes were my only chance at maintaining a life/work balance.

With a great sigh, I tossed the stack of papers down onto the coffee table and took a sip of room-temperature coffee from the mug my mom bought me. The mug was a gift to celebrate the start of a "new chapter" and was decorated in pastel strawberries. The seeds of the strawberries were painted in a rising glaze, giving the berries a neat texture that I enjoyed rubbing with my thumb.

"How's work?" my mom asked.

"Fine," I said.

"Well that's good, right?"

"Sure," I said.

Since my return to Colorado the week before, most of our conversations followed that script. Questions followed by short answers. I knew she was trying to reconnect with me since everything that happened, but I also knew that she thought she saved me. And since I didn't want to lie anymore, I held on to what I really wanted to say. It was painful to see my mom so sad about the disconnection between us. She was trying so hard to love me.

* * *

Carlos Garcia was the very best boss I ever worked for. Maybe it was his patience with me, or the way he didn't let how tired he was get in the way of anything. The man used to come over to the house all the time to hang out with my dad, but I never really got to know him until I started working at Creekside Memorial & Cremation.

At first, the work consisted of trivial and repetitive tasks, like vacuuming the viewing rooms or dusting the showroom caskets. As a new hire, I was expected to assist on all removals, embalmings, and cremations for the first month. This meant that as soon as Carlos or Robin were called for a body removal, I was called too. Several – if not most – of the calls happened between midnight and four in the morning. Slave to insomnia, I was averaging two to three hours of sleep each night, so I was thankful for the nights when no one died, and I could wake up on my own time.

Embalmings were typically done during the day if we could help it. I was slow to learn the process, but by the time the leaves started changing, I was a pro. Carlos had a lot to say about the good job I was doing, and Robin constantly complimented me. Together, they made me out to be a prodigy, but I didn't feel like I was anything special. I was just the same, sad kid I was before California, only with people to miss. I was back in old patterns, and I will say, watching leaves change without changing with them was hard.

Once a week, I was to wax and polish the hearse and town car. Only after I joined Robin, the thirty-something mortician from Kansas, on several funeral processions would I be allowed to drive the hearse. But since I still hated driving, I preferred to stay back with Carlos when possible. As I watched Carlos work, the conversation would fade in and out of instructions and stories, and I found myself captivated by his insight. He understood people. Carlos knew society's pitfalls and could hold a conversation with anyone, almost like he had the human equation all figured out.

I was exhausted that first year, but Carlos was always there to talk me through it. By the start of the second year, I was able to go on removals, embalm, cremate, meet with families, and arrange funerals all on my own. Robin was glad, too, because we were finally able to balance the workload equally. She and I would handle the removals and most of the embalmings and cremations, while Carlos managed the accounting and finances. All of us met with the families and helped each other when needed.

Robin and I agreed, though, that Carlos shouldn't lift any more bodies. He was in his late fifties and suffered from a handful of health problems – one of which being a major respiratory condition that he didn't let on about. I only knew about it because Robin told me.

Robin McClay was the daughter of a surgeon. She only ever spoke about her dad, but I later learned that when Robin was eight years old, her mom was found dead in her car. All Robin was willing to say about it was, "She did it to herself."

"That's why she wanted to do this," Carlos told me. He started coughing, which broke my heart. "But she knows anatomy, so she's a good fit." Carlos, who took over his family's business after his dad died, found his way to it out of necessity. His brother Eric had left for New Mexico, so without Carlos stepping up to run it, the funeral home would have ended on its sixth generation. After getting to know Carlos, I think he would have rather done something else, but careers are hard to leave thirty years later.

Carlos was the only one helped me move into the apartments on the corner of 12th and Acacia. He knew that I was nervous as hell to meet my roommate and had a hefty number of boxes to move. "Don't let him lift anything," Robin said, but I wasn't going to let him do anything other than chat. I told him he could bring over whatever didn't fit in my little yellow truck as long as I loaded it. Between his truck and mine, we were able to move all of it in one trip.

Keith, the college sophomore I should not have been nervous *at all* to move in with, did not like me. I didn't care, though, because I didn't like him either. After a month or two of forced small talk, we each silently resolved to keep to ourselves. It was during that same autumn that I began taking online classes, so I converted half of my room into an office. That way, I could focus on schoolwork and leave the living room to the religiously coked-up Keith and his fake friends.

For my twenty-first birthday, Carlos got me a large bottle of his favorite whiskey. He, Robin, and I all took shots of it at the end of the day and toasted in silence. The next day, I went down to the courthouse and was is-sued an updated driver's license; one with a new picture and current address. I was told to take off my glasses for the photo. My eyesight got worse over the last year and half, and I couldn't get by without them. I wasn't alarmed by it, having worn reading glasses for most of my life, but now glasses were part of my forever face.

Next to the picture was my name, Ian Marlow, and the descriptions of my identifying features – green eyes, blond hair, my height (five foot, nine inches), and my weight. My biology was casually listed next to a handful of numbers and dates, and my name was still "Ian" – the man I was – and not "Lemon," the man I so badly wanted to be.

I won't say I blamed my alcoholism on his death, but not having Carlos around was the last push into loneliness I could take. Alli hadn't tried to reach out once since I left California two years ago, but I didn't try to call her either. I was too embarrassed about how I treated Kelly, so I let that friendship rot as well. And I had to accept that I wasn't going to hear from Andrew. He was back to living a version of his life that Lemon didn't exist in, and I was doing the same.

With no one around to lie to, I told lies to myself instead. Lies like, *I can take care of myself* and *I love myself the way I am.* Drinking made the lies more real. I guess that's why so many people fall into it – liquor, weed, coke, whatever; loneliness is the only gateway drug. I was never drunk at work, but I made up for it in the evenings when I didn't have to try nearly as hard to make myself throw up.

<h1 align="center">15</h1>

I met Carlos' daughter, Caitlyn, and his twin sons Rob and Chuck at the funeral. Though the three siblings shared a father, that seemed to be the only commonality between them.

Caitlyn and her husband flew out from New York, but only stayed for the service. Rob and his wife Emily were both thirty-eight years old and had three kids, one of which had to be scolded several times to stop plucking petals from the flower arrangements. The five of them traveled almost as far as Caitlyn and her husband did, but they wouldn't return to Washington D.C. until after the weekend. Chuck, who was single and without children, spent most of the time before and after the service chatting with Robin and me about our former boss.

"He used to want me to take over the business," said Chuck. "But after I moved to Florida, he gave up on that. I felt bad for a while, but it helped us both, I think."

"Oh yeah?" I asked, staring at the bare orchid plant gripped by Caitlyn and Rob's youngest.

"Well, he was finally able to see me as a son and not as a business partner."

"Oh," I said. "So, who–"

"But you two will do great, I can tell."

"Us?"

"Yeah," said Chuck. "Congrats."

Robin and I stood in shock as the tall Chuck rejoined his siblings. "There's no way," Robin said, but sure enough, an attorney was on our doorstep the next morning with fast words and a stack of documents. His name was Ryan and he loved his job (as far as I could tell). One of the documents was a handwritten letter from Carlos describing how Creekside Memorial & Cremation was to be transferred over to Robin and me as co-owners.

"I'm so, so sorry it's so late in the game for this, but we had to wait for his kids to go through it all first, y'know?" I was impressed by Ryan's ability to fit all of his words in one breath.

"No yeah, I get it," I said and began filling the spaces next to Robin's initials with my own. In a moment, I was the co-owner of a funeral home. Stuck.

By the end of its first year, the Marlow & McClay Mortuary had new carpet throughout, updated viewing areas, a much larger garage for the new fleet of transport vans, brand-new embalming equipment, and a fresh coat of brilliant maroon paint on the exterior.

There was enough money left in the business account to cover the renovations, but I paid for most of them myself since I had nothing better to do with my money than paint the walls with it. I was better at saving my money – a skill learned very quickly when handed half of a business – but it didn't change how I felt about it. Instead, I kept a few consistent hundred on a debit card and the rest as cash in a small safe in my bedroom closet.

Around that same time – a few months after I turned twenty-three – my parents sold my childhood home in the name of downsizing. I hadn't lived there in years and didn't have any say in the matter anyway, but I was still living in the small apartment with Keith and would have put my own offer down on it if I knew.

"We sold it privately," my dad said, "so we could get more for it. People from New York are used to paying too much for things anyway." Hearing this made me realize that even if I were to put an offer on the house I grew up in, they would have expected me to pay as much as a stranger would.

* * *

Since it was just us two, Robin and I came up with a simple work schedule. The funeral home was closed on the weekends, so we each chose one of the five weekdays to take off. One of us was always on-call, though, in case something happened in the middle of the night or over the weekend – we traded that responsibility back and forth each week.

Robin called me on a Friday – my day off – to ask for help with an embalming. This happened now and then, if there were difficult cases, so I didn't think anything of it. I grabbed my jacket and drove down to the mortuary.

When I got there, Robin was draped over the front desk with her head cradled in the nest of her crossed arms.

"You okay?" I asked.

She lifted her head. I could tell she had been crying, so I didn't say anything else. Even though it was our job, there was no getting over the periodic cases that snagged our humanity. I let Robin alone and drifted slowly to the embalming room.

Embalming was more ritual than routine. Yes, there was a precise procedure to follow, but I felt that there was metrical ceremony in turning flesh into plastic. I set out two bottles of synthetic pink toxicant, checked the clock, and got to work.

Traditional embalming regalia consisted of a full body gown, rubber gloves, and a face mask, all of which incorporated an unrestricted, wintergreen mint. I put my gloves on last. While washing her corpse, I surveyed the condition of the woman's body to determine the correct ratio of embalming fluids. I noticed other things about her, though, and quickly realized what made Robin call me.

The woman on the table was tall and in her mid-thirties. There was very little muscle that clung to her framework, and her lips were thin and chapped. Her fingernails were chewed all the way down past her fingertips, caused by irreputable stress and fatigue. Around her chin and brow were clusters of small sores, and the bruising on the bend of her left arm confirmed that the life-taker was the heroin floating in her stagnant veins.

With a modest twist of stainless-steel, a stream of water came steadily from the faucet above the woman's shoulders so that all proof of former vitality would be rinsed away. I made a small opening in the tissue near the clavicle and secured the give-and-take into the artery and vein. Her eyes and mouth were secured by glue and wire so that when the synthetic vibrancy of life filled her cheeks, she wouldn't look like a corpse at all.

With all flesh prepared and equipment secured, I turned on the machine and allowed noxious conserve to replace the blood in her body. The machine thumped on while I flexed the corpse's major joints. Lastly, I repositioned her hands so that they laid across her mid waist, interlocking her thumbs. Right hand on top.

I didn't expect Robin to stay, so she startled me when she knocked on the door. "She looks like a mermaid," I said, watching the woman's long, brunette curls sway in the current.

Robin leaned against the wall. "My mom was a mermaid too."

* * *

I heard my phone ringing on the dresser near my bed, but I ignored it. I was in the middle of the last writing assignment of my pointless student career and didn't have time for anything else. The living room I shared a wall with was filled with people from Keith's world who yelled out the lyrics to whatever song was playing, and that was obnoxious enough.

Robin offered to take the on-call phone for another week so I could finish the semester on a high note. I told her I would be on-call two weeks in a row after, to keep it fair, but I planned on getting her a gift card as way of thanking her.

My phone rang again; its obnoxious vibrations pulsing through the floor. I waited through three of the rings before I finally went over to it. When I saw the name on the screen, I immediately threw it up to my ear.

"Hey Ian," the voice sighed through the phone. It was Alli.

"Hey."

"Ian, um." Alli paused. It was the same way I paused when I had to tell someone the last thing they wanted to hear.

"Is it Aunt Lou?" I asked.

"No, Ian, it's Andrew, he...he's dead, Ian, I only just found out."

Dull breaths were hoisted up through my gut and into the part of my heart where his love was kept. My pulse was severed, and it surged out in waves of painful, mutilated novae while I clutched the back of my chair in a white-knuckle grip. Blaring music from the other room echoed in the hollowness of mine, and I didn't even feel my elbow hit the bed frame when I slumped to the floor.

"Ian?"

"I'm here," I said between heaves. I didn't want to know how it happened, so I didn't ask. Instead, I said, "When's the funeral?"

"Saturday."

"I'll be there," I said and hung up.

16

My memories and the people in them drift back into the parts of my subconscious I think they belong to. The flight is over and all I want to do is to get to my hotel room.

"You can leave it open," the flight attendant says as I start to close the overhead bin. I nod awkwardly and file in line behind the woman with the cheetah-print neck pillow.

I easily find my way out of the airport and onto the hotel shuttle. With my bag on my lap, I type out a quick text to Alli letting her know that I'm back in San Diego. I will see her at the funeral tomorrow, but I don't have it in me to see anyone before then. Out the windows of the shuttle, I watch the world of San Diego revolving around me, and I feel consumed by it. The sun and glass reflect my face at me, and I hate recognizing the youth I killed off. *Maybe I'm just hungry,* I think, but I know I'm just tired of remembering the things that overwhelm me.

I almost trip, wasting no time between getting off the shuttle and checking into my hotel room. The man at the front desk asks me to confirm my name, among other pointless things like my date of birth and when I plan to check out again.

"Ian Marlow," I say, to which he only nods and hands me the plastic key to room 413. I grab a fistful of jellybeans from the dish on the counter, accidentally dropping a few of them on the floor. The clerk pretends not to notice, so I do too.

Plants, mostly tropical, fill the lobby. I take a deep breath and wander around the hotel lobby crowd toward the elevators. My room is on the fourth floor. Unlucky.

In my room, I set out the clothes I bought for the funeral and call Robin who has no idea that I'm in California. I am still no good at explaining things like this.

"Wait, what? Why are you-"

"For a funeral, Robin, it's for a funeral."

"Oh, um, okay. Is it family?"

I say, "something like that" and fidget with the bracelet.

"I guess I'll see you Sunday?"

"Yep. Sunday."

Robin hangs up. She's not thrilled, I can tell, but I don't care. I'm in a different world now, and I can't handle it, honestly. I haven't cried yet, but there is no pulse in my candy heart. It's in chalky pieces, so I decide to find the nearest bar and get drunk about it.

Everything about San Diego is somehow the same, but the pulse is slower. People passing me on the street seem suspended in a strange otherworldliness that I can't be a part of. Maybe I am the stagnant one, and the world is pulsing around me in ways I can't recognize – not yet. People take more pictures now, and I appreciate that. For the most part, conversations sound the same. Busy sidewalks filled with strangers who have no idea why they are who they are, and I am a stranger seated at some bar a few blocks from the hotel watching other strangers through the glass. I feel like an octopus.

"Just a tequila shot," I say to the thin, hairy bartender with glasses like mine. "Nice glasses."

"Oh, thanks," he replies and grabs the expensive bottle. He pours a shining shot of liquid gold into the small glass. Like all things, ceremony is absolute. "That'll be seven bucks."

I pull my debit card out of my pocket and slide it to him. "Can I run a tab?"

"Sure, man, no problem."

Yeah, there's no problem, I lie to myself and make the tequila vanish. I set the empty shot glass in front of the bartender and nod. As he pours the second shot, I scan the bar for hopelessness I can relate to.

There is a woman in blue pointing out the daisies on her shirt to a man in green shoes. He likes her, I think. From what I can tell, they've known each other long enough to know whether or not the daisies will stay on her shoulder or end up in a shared pile of laundry. *His socks are probably green too,* I think. *His socks are probably green.*

Away from the bar, by the far end of the long room, there's a keyboard and drum kit. I hope someone does something with it because there is no rhythmic noise in the bar, only side conversations and clunky glass. I roll my eyes. I ask for another shot of tequila and a man's voice calls to me from in front of the green shoes and daisies.

"Do you play?" he says.

"What?" I ask the glossy-eyed man at the table. He has a friendly melancholy about him, and I swear his wedding ring is tattooed on. I don't even mind that his shirt is stained, or that the sunglasses perched on the top of his head are missing one of their lenses. It is the sudden self-insertion that startles me.

"Do you play?"

"Play what?"

"Chess." He gestures down to the chessboard that is sitting in front of him, but without making a show of it.

"Sometimes," I say, then ask the bartender for a third or forth dose.

"Is right now a 'sometime?'"

"Uuuuh, are you inviting me to play?"

"If you're up for it."

I think about it for a moment, trying to decide if I should ignore him and go back to my own mind, or get over myself and play into it. *So what,* I think and am up and moving toward the sticky table to play chess with a stranger. And since no one likes drinking alone, I buy a dose of tequila for him too.

Some local up-and-comers take to the keyboard and drumkit while I make the first move – my rightmost knight over the line of pawns and one square to the left. He moves one of the pawns on his right side up two spaces, which I mirror with a pawn on my own side. As we move and trade pieces, sighing and cursing when our favorites are taken, we make small talk. It's hard to hear each other over the live band in the corner, but we manage. And as we play, this stranger and I lose ourselves in tequila.

"Name's Tim," he says. "What's yours?"

"Ian," I mumble through my drunk.

"Sorry, my hearing's shit. What is it?"

"Lemon," I holler at him, remembering that I can be whoever the hell I want to be when talking to strangers. "I'm only here for th' weeken'." Tim is handling the five tequila shots way better than I am, but to be fair, I had two before I came to play chess.

"People actually call you that?" he asks.

"Nickname."

"Oh ya?"

"Yeah, sure."

"What brings you to town?"

"Renonovotor, wait, no...*renovating* my dad's place." I throw my arms out wide and say, "He's got this huuuuuge house, man, it's huge! And his wi- no, his *husband* just trashed the place. Tore th' whole fucking thing up, I guess. So now, now I havtuh fucking fix it!"

Tim is stuck with an appalled look on his face, but he's not looking at me. Instead, his eyes are fixed on the server I doused in cold beer behind me.

"I am so sorry," I say, trying to stand up.

Tim says "It's okay, I got it," and rises from his seat to help the hops-soaked waiter who has glasses just like mine. Only now, in this light, I realize that our glasses aren't the same at all. They just have a similar shape. My glasses are a rich forest green, but his are a deep navy. I turn from the scene I caused and rest my chin in my hand. My eyes blink slower than I want them to, and I can feel the nectar under my eyelids thicken with each pass. The live band is playing something slow, but I can't pay attention well enough to hear the words right now.

"Whose move?" Tim asks, sitting back down across the board.

I say "yours" and watch Tim move his only bishop down toward my leftmost pawn. I was waiting for this. In a casual way, I move my rook six squares to the left, landing it in direct line with his king. My knight is placed perfectly a few spaces over, preventing Tim from moving his king out of the way. And even though one of his pawns is blocking my bishop, there's nothing he can do about the trap in its entirety.

Tim stares down at the board and its pieces, realizing in full that there is no way out of it. "Dammit."

17

The alarm I set for 7:30 a.m. is still going off, and I fight the urge to push the snooze button a second time. My sheets are damp with sweat, matching the damp air of my hotel room. It's not hot in the room, though, because I accidentally left the window open all night and I had been sweating for choices. *I'll start cutting back,* I think, but I've been recycling that lie long enough to know that it will only last a week at the most, then I'll be right back to my death grip habit.

Groggy and slow, I peel myself out of my hotel bed and walk naked to the coffee pot on the counter by the television. The game show channel I fell asleep to last night has since switched over to some morning talk show where the guest speaker is going on and on about opinions of the climate. I dig the remote out from under the bed covers and turn off the noise.

The room smells like coffee; a bitter morning drenched in stains and percolated numbness. I don't even like coffee, but it's all I have right now to get moving, and I don't have the time to think too long about options. As it brews, I get dressed without even looking in a mirror until after I'm fully clothed.

Underwear first, then pants. A gray button up shirt with thin pinstripes drapes over my torso while I roll up my sleeves. My black belt keeps my shirt and pants in tandem while I hunch over to put my socks. Finally, I secure my shape with a waistcoat – my new favorite way to hide my body – and slip on my shoes. Tightening the strap in the back of my waistcoat, I admire the taper between my torso and my waist.

The bracelet Andrew gave me is secure on my wrist. I try once more to come up with more ways to honor the memory of Andrew, but I can't hang out on top of buildings with him anymore.

I find the handwritten list I had been carrying around for the last twenty-four hours and toss it in the trash. It lands somewhere between tissues and plastic water cups, and I understand, all at once, how thankful I am that I won't have to see Andrew's body. He would be in a pine box or cremated, sitting in a marble or oak urn. Or maybe he followed through with the whole "becoming a tree" thing. Regardless, he wouldn't be embalmed, so no chance of an open casket. The tattoo near his shoulder told me that.

I call Alli on my way to the funeral. I don't have a reason for it, but I need something to do during the 20-minute drive that isn't staring out the window avoiding emotionality.

"You ready for this?" she asks.

"I don't know, I think so."

"His grandpa's here."

"Really?"

"Yep."

"Why?"

"No idea."

Guilt – the one true thing that separates humans from the other earth-wandering beasts. Memories keep us going most of the time, but we are forced to remember the other stuff too. The stuff that hurts the most because you know that no matter what, you can't go back and do anything about it. Flowers, stones, and animals don't have to carry guilt and can live their lives not regretting the way they treat each other. But they don't get the memories either, so maybe it's for the best. Memories and guilt serve as foundations for human experience, and I have plenty of both.

I pull into the mostly full parking lot and step out of the car. Trying to only focus on one thought at a time, I recognize right away the smell of the sea as the breeze from the west glides over my face and neck. The beach is maybe a few blocks away.

Alli is standing by the main doors like she said she would be. She's in a sleek black dress with bishop sleeves that billow to her midarm, just past her elbow. Her hair is pulled back into a tight braid that drapes on her shoulder. Alli's signature aviator sunglasses complete the mourner-chic.

"You look nice," she said, and through the tone of her voice, it sounds like she's happy to see me. I'm happy to see her too, but I can't tell if it's because she is a friendly distraction from everything going on in my mind. Nervous, I slip a peppermint into my mouth.

"Do your folks know you're here?" she asks.

"No, but they've been in the mountains all week, so they wouldn't have gotten my call anyway."

"*Would* you have called?"

"No."

"Ian..."

"Let's get going," I say, and we step off of the burning asphalt and into the air-conditioned mortuary where a stout, elderly man is handing out memorial cards printed on maroon paper. Andrew's youthful face stands out against the background. I slide the card into my back pocket and follow Alli into the viewing room.

Everyone in the room seems naturally divided into two main groups – coworkers and friends – and I don't know which group I belong to. Carol, Yaryna, and the others stand in a haphazard way, chatting. I wonder if Carol still feels bad for firing Andrew. Probably. Hopefully. No, that's mean of me.

Kayla and her husband Dillan are here too, sitting next to two empty seats with Alli's handbag thrown over the back of one and a jacket over the other. I wave to Kayla, and she waves back. Dillan doesn't see me yet because he's looking at the crowd at the front of the room. I notice the crowd, too, and will probably join it soon to look at whatever endearing display was set up to honor Andrew. There are tears in my eyes, but I'm letting them fall now.

Drifting around and keeping to myself, I recognize the man in the front row wearing black jeans and a blue-striped button-down shirt as the one who once routinely beat the king of California. I hadn't seen a picture of him, but I can tell by the way the room is moving around him that the man in the front row is Andrew's grandfather.

Before today, I would have shunned this man; maybe told him how fucked up it was to give up on someone like Andrew. But no matter how I try to twist it around in my mind, I am no better than him. We share a common guilt, and that's a rare thing. For different reasons, sure, but I also gave up on Andrew, and that is enough to make me want to talk to his grandfather.

"Sorry, do I know you?" he asks. My outstretched hand goes unshaken. The peppermint in my mouth is slow to dissolve.

"No, but I knew Andrew."

"I'm sure everyone here knew him. That's why they came."

I pull my hand back in and take the seat next to him. I hear him scoff, but I don't let it get to me. I don't understand why I'm doing this, but I want his company. We sit for a while in silence, staring at the floor and memorial cards until he finally says, "How?"

"S-sorry. How?"

"How did you know him?" he says, sternly. I think of how to reply as the old man looks away from me and at baseboard trim instead, which is painted in a coral pink that stands out against the deep green wallpaper. *Just say you worked with him,* I think, but that would leave a truth unlived. I understand that now.

"I love him," I say, for the first time out loud in any form. "We loved each other."

"Give me a break," the old man says, rolling his eyes and coughing into a balled-up fist.

I say "Fine," and leave the man alone in the row of empty chairs. The crowd near the front dissipates as people take their seats, so I take the opportunity to approach the front. As I get closer, though, my spirits sink. "No," I whisper to myself, under hot breath. My feet stop moving and my voice shakes. "No, no."

At the front of the room, nestled between potent lilies and winding ferns is a casket of brushed steel and fine satin. And in the casket is the embalmed body of Andrew Reyes.

I stumble forward, eyes wide and red-faced. Resting my hands on the edge of the metal box, I can feel my hot blood in my fingers.

Andrew's face seems warm and kinetic, as if his mouth would open at any moment to speak subtle and worldly words. His arms are straight at his sides, but his chest does not rise and fall like the Andrew I knew. This Andrew is full of life in looks only, like a doll of a man. New in the box. Plastic.

I lean over and discreetly unbutton Andrew's shirt. I need to see the proof of it: a two-inch long baseball stitch carving through what used to be a tattoo. The funeral director notices, so I cover the stitch back up and step back.

"Is everything all right, sir?"

"Why is he like this?" I ask, using my sleeve to wipe the sweat from the side of my face. He knows why I asked, so he takes his time answering. I chomp up the rest of the peppermint and swallow the shards. My teeth chatter.

"For the comfort of the family, sir."

"Don't bullshit me, I know he didn't want this."

"Sir, like I said, it was for–"

"No," I say. "I know how this works. Thi-this is wrong. He didn't want this."

"There was nothing in writing, so his next of kin made the arrangements."

"*Him!?*" I erupt, pointing across the room to the old man who, in my mind, should be in the box and not Andrew. Everyone else in the room is looking at me; all holding their breath and tongues.

"Sir," the jaded man continues, "I'm going to ask you to ple–"

"He's supposed to be a tree!" I yell. "He wanted to be a tree, don't you understand!? He told me he wanted to be a tree!"

The man is scared of me. No one in the room moves. Alli has her hand over her mouth, and I am standing way too close to the flowers.

Alli moves toward me and the man steps back. "Ian, let's ju–"

"You know what?" I say, "fuck this," and leave down the center aisle of chairs, past Alli and the rest of the Gilded Naupakas. Alli follows, trying to calm me down, but she knows I just don't work that way. Alli starts to yell the wrong name at me, so I start running. Soon, Alli's yelling will be drowned out by the noise of the neighborhood.

The parking lot and its mortuary grow smaller as I sprint through avenues, crosswalks, and neighborhoods, and I finally make it to where the real people are. They wander the coast on their unassuming boardwalks and beaches while small waves thump against the sand.

Being as far west as I can be, I fall to the sand and cry.

I lift my wrist and count the artificial gemstones that clung to it. Sixty-three cubic zirconia pieces dismantling the light on a metal chain, and they're heavy because I can see a different version of my face in each stone. Almost all of me is made up of things I have to lie about, or think I have to lie about, just to keep the wrong people comfortable. I used to be worried that my hands weren't big enough to hold heavy things, but they are, and I've been holding heavy things for too long. Heavy things, like candy in my pockets, joyous sex, unclaimed aquarium tickets, and the realization that I am the only one who withheld the life I wanted because I made the wrong choice on purpose.

I rip the authentic replication – the real fake – from my wrist and hurl it into the waves.

After

I'm in the mirror and I am naked. This is no longer my routine, but I just took a shower, and it had been a while since I last surveyed the way I look. Turning slowly, I view myself at every possible angle. My forty-one-year-old body has a different shape than it did before, but my mind has changed too. I love the way I look, and I love the way I think.

My chest is round, mostly, but there is muscle there that defines the two halves of my chest as separate from each other. My lower gut lacks definition and sticks out a little further than my chest. I put my hands on my hips, resting them where my obliques used to be. From what I can tell, I am doing a pretty good job maintaining a healthy weight.

I can't help fixating on the hair on my legs, but I've come to accept that, like many things, the bald spot behind my right calf was never going to disappear. In fact, it's grown bigger now, as my body hair has thinned out. The hair on my head has thinned a bit too, but my hairline is more or less the same. The hair on my face is thick, though, and a full beard with gray in its fringes frames my face without extending too far off my chin.

Kind eyes, green like beetle wings, observe the human form in front of the mirror. Every dip and bend and crease in my flesh are the pieces of a machine, and I am glad that it can still move and grow. All of this breath, pulse, and beat for a determined lacework of nerves and veins? Absolutely.

I've watched a lot of things change, but I am grateful for what hasn't. I still have all of my teeth, and cobalt blue is still my favorite color. I also love the rain as much as ever, and I'm still young enough to run out into it in a pair of gym shorts. Usually, I run back inside laughing and happy to be in a world where I can still catch my breath. I'm so lucky it worked out this way.

I continue my midmorning contemplations while getting dressed and wonder if my mom will remember to call. Her sister, who she moved in with after the divorce, might have to remind her that today is Tuesday.

My mom has called me on my birthday for the last thirteen years. She's in her seventies now, and that once guaranteed call has since become a call I can only hope for. But we talk often enough that if I had to pretend my birthday was on a Wednesday this year, I wouldn't mind.

When my dad cheated on my mom the third time, it didn't matter who it was with. My mom decided she was done dealing with it, so she divorced him and asked her family in Chicago for a place to stay. It was a shot in the dark, but they embraced her. I've flown out a few times to visit. They're good people. And though my mom never remarried, she enjoys the person she has become on her own. I'm so proud of her for that.

My dad and I don't speak to each other, which means I haven't spoken to him since I called my parents to tell them that I was at a funeral in California, and that I wouldn't be coming home. Of course, that was a heavy blow to land on the ones who raised me, but it needed to be done. They hung up on me. Two years later, my mom called to tell me about the divorce and asked to salvage whatever we could of our relationship. I paid for her ticket to see me.

Without anyone to shift blame to, my dad changed his number and started over with new people. All I know is that he bought a house in Maine and lives there with his third wife. I can't remember her name. I've never met her.

Alli has offered to visit several times, but I prefer flying down to Florida to visit her instead. After Aunt Lou died, Alli sold her home in North Park and moved to a small coastal town in the gulf where she bartends full-time. The beachside bar she opened exclusively uses her homemade tequila.

My dad did not attend Aunt Lou's funeral, which was a surprise to no one. Kayla and Dillan were there, though, and it was great to reconnect with them both.

Kayla asked about the tarot reading she gave me, wondering if I had come to any realizations about the lobster and balance. I nodded and pulled down my shirt collar to show off the small lobster tattoo on the left side of my neck. Lobsters, with claws or otherwise, have come to mean a great deal to me. No one really knows the true lifespan of a lobster. The same is true for the moments in our own lives. Moments that we could never know how long they would have lasted because we ended them too soon. Lobsters are moments.

I walk to the front door and slide the glass down, revealing the screen. I'll do the same with the backdoor so that the breeze from the sea can move freely through my house and take anything stagnant with it. Not before tea, though.

I place the strawberry mug my mom gave me on the counter by the sink and choose a bag of peppermint tea from the selection in the pantry. My teapot has lemons on it, but I won it in a raffle, so it's purely coincidental. I put it on the back burner of the stove and wait for either boiling water or my phone to ring – I'll focus on whatever comes first.

On the fridge in my kitchen are some artifacts that mean the world to me, and I would never consider getting rid of them. Some of Andrew's poetry, a plane ticket from my trip to Greece, and the handwritten letter from Kelly – all proudly held by souvenir magnets. I didn't think I would want to save Kelly's letter, but here it is after all this time. She forgave me for the way I acted, even though she didn't have to and wouldn't have ever known how much it meant to me to cry happy sobs with her over the phone. I told her *everything.*

Getting over the grief of Andrew was difficult, but I made it through. And though I didn't get the chance to say it at his funeral, I did tell Andrew that I loved him when I revisited Joshua Tree National Park a year after. The desert is the best place to see the edge of the world, and as unusual as it would seem to strangers watching, I didn't want to be anyone other than myself shouting "I love you!" at the stars because I knew he was one of them.

When my daughter is older, I will tell her why I chose to stay in California and why her name is Andrea. It was selfish of me to name her after him, but it was important to me that he gets to be a part of whatever amazing things she does. For now, though, I will watch from my kitchen window as she picks oranges from the tree in our backyard. I hope she loves herself more than I was able to at her age, and I hope she knows how much she means to me. These are heavy things, I know, but I made room for them already.

So, it's just us two, the Marlows, in our single-story house in San Francisco. It rains more often in San Francisco than the other places I considered living, and I didn't already have memories here. I'm a sentimental person, but not to the point of living somewhere on sentiment alone. There was no way I could live in San Diego. I visit now and then, though.

And when I'm there, I make sure to wander down the boardwalk at Ocean Beach to see for myself the sign that asks *WHERE ARE YOU FROM?* in large, red letters. Pressed into the map is a purple pushpin that marks where Andrew and I watched the world from a rooftop. Home.

Acknowledgments

I would like to thank David for his irreplaceable guidance, endless support, and unparalleled love. My gratitude also extends to Ana, Dänya, Leeanne, and my parents Jenny and Stephen Sr. for the various ways they have contributed to the fulfillment of this dream.

You all mean the world to me.

Stephen Mathews writes to showcase the moments in life that define the individual. His experiences as a funeral director, journalist, and English Language Arts instructor have given Stephen a unique appreciation for what makes us human. He and his husband David live and work in Colorado, but regardless of occupation, Stephen will always write.